HEARTLAND™

Coming Home

Read all the books about Heartland:

Coming Home
Lauren Brooke

■SCHOLASTIC

Picture of Warrior courtesy of Vauxhall City Farm.
For more information visit www.vauxhallcityfarm.org

Scholastic Children's Books
An imprint of Scholastic Ltd
Euston House, 24 Eversholt Street
London, NW1 1DB, UK
Registered office: Westfield Road, Southam, Warwickshire, CV47 0RA
SCHOLASTIC and associated logos are trademarks and
or registered trademarks of Scholastic Inc.
Series created by Working Partners

First published in the UK by Scholastic Ltd, 2000
This edition published 2009

Text copyright © Working Partners, 2000

ISBN 978 1407 11159 9

British Library Cataloguing-in-Publication Data
A CIP catalogue record for this book is available from the British Library

The right of Lauren Brooke to be identified as the author of this work has been asserted by her.

Printed in the UK by CPI Group (UK) Ltd, Croydon, CR0 4YY
Papers used by Scholastic Children's Books are made from wood grown in
sustainable forests.

3 5 7 8 10 8 6 4

This is a work of fiction. Names, characters, places, incidents and dialogues are products of the
author's imagination or are used fictitiously. Any resemblance to actual people, living or dead,
events or locales is entirely coincidental.

www.scholastic.co.uk/zone

With special thanks to Linda Chapman

With thanks to Monty Roberts, who first wrote about the "join-up" technique and whose work has made the world a better place for horses

For Craig Walker — who listened and understood

Chapter One

As the school bus disappeared into the distance, Amy Fleming shifted her rucksack on to her shoulder and set off up the long driveway that led to Heartland. On either side of the dusty track were fields filled with horses and ponies grazing lazily in the afternoon sunshine, their tails swishing away the clouds of flies that buzzed around them. Amy smiled. It was a sight that always made her feel glad to be home.

She hurried on up the curving driveway towards the weather-boarded house and brick stable block with its whitewashed doors. As she drew near, one of the stall doors opened and Ty, Heartland's seventeen-year-old stable-hand, came out leading Copper, a chestnut gelding.

Amy waved, but Ty was concentrating on the horse and didn't see her. He led him up past the turn-out paddocks towards the circular training ring at the top of the yard. Amy shaded her eyes. She could just make out the slim, blonde figure of her mom waiting at the gate.

Amy hurried past the farmhouse and up the track after Ty. There was nothing she loved more than watching her mom at work and it looked like she was about to start a session with Copper.

As Ty drew the horse to a halt near the gate, the gelding threw his head up to dislodge the flies settling on his face. Automatically, Ty put a hand up to brush the flies away. With a sudden loud whinny of alarm, Copper shot backwards.

"Copper!" Amy gasped as the horse reared, his front hooves flailing in the air.

"Whoa!" Ty cried, stumbling in surprise.

Copper's front hooves clattered down to the ground. The whites of his eyes showed his panic. Ty managed to grab the lead-rope but the sudden movement sent the terrified horse rearing up again, his lethal hooves whisking through the air only centimetres away from Ty's head.

"Here!" Marion Fleming's voice rang out. The next instant she was by Ty's side, grabbing the lead-rope from him. "Steady, now! Steady!" she called to the horse.

Momentarily landing on the ground, Copper reared straight up again. Holding on lightly to the end of the lead-rope, Marion let him go. Amy watched her mother intently. Her lips were moving in soothing words as she calmed the frightened creature.

Copper came down with a snort and then reared again

but this time not as high. Still Marion talked. Copper's hooves came crashing down, but this time he stood still with all four feet on the ground, trembling slightly. For a long second Marion didn't move, her eyes fixed on his, her voice calming and reassuring. As he relaxed she turned her body at a slight angle to his and moved slowly towards him, her eyes averted. Amy held her breath. As Marion reached for Copper's halter he snorted and lowered his head.

Amy let out a huge sigh of relief.

Ty's face was pale. "I can't believe I was so stupid!" he exclaimed, pushing a hand through his dark hair.

Marion looked round. "It's OK, Ty," she said. "It was just a mistake. You forgot what Copper's like about hands around his head." She patted the horse. "And with good cause," she added.

Amy knew what she meant. Copper had come to Heartland four weeks ago, a ruined show horse whose owners had been reported for beating him around the head with a whip after he had knocked a series of jumps down. Slowly, under Marion's care, Copper was regaining his trust in humans.

For the first time, Amy's mom seemed to notice her. "Hi, honey!" she said, a smile lighting up her blue eyes. "Had a good day at school?"

"Sure," Amy said. She didn't want to talk about school. "Is Copper OK?" she asked, hurrying forward.

"He'll be fine," Marion said, leading him into the ring. "I'm going to join-up with him. Want to watch?"

"You bet!" Amy answered eagerly. She went and stood beside Ty at the gate. "Hi," she said, dumping her bag on the floor.

"Hi there," Ty replied. His hair flopped down across his forehead as he looked at her, his green eyes portraying self-disgust. "I guess you saw that."

Amy knew he was talking about Copper's panic. She nodded.

"I can't believe I tried to brush those flies away like that, Amy," Ty said, shaking his head. "How dumb can you get?"

"Don't worry," she said reassuringly, putting her arms over the top of the gate and nudging him. "Look at him now."

Amy watched intently, momentarily lost in what she was seeing. Copper was cantering freely around the ring in smooth circles, his hooves thudding rhythmically on the sand surface. Marion Fleming stood in the middle of the ring. No rope or line attached horse to human but it was as if they were bound by an invisible thread. As her mom moved a step forward in line with the gelding's head, Copper slowed – as she moved back, he quickened up. The horse's outside ear was pricked forward but his inside ear was riveted on the person in the centre. He stretched out his head and neck, his nostrils blowing at the ground. He was saying that he trusted her.

Amy glanced at Ty. He met her gaze and they exchanged smiles. "There's nothing like seeing your mom work," he said quietly. "If I could be just one tenth as good with horses, I'd be happy."

"Me too," Amy sighed.

Marion urged Copper on. And then, after two more circuits, the horse started to open and shut his mouth as if he was chewing. Amy knew that it was the signal her mom had been waiting for. She watched as her mother turned her body sideways on to the horse and waited. The gelding slowed and stopped. He looked towards the centre. Amy held her breath. Would he decide to join-up with Marion? There was a second's pause and then Copper walked over to Marion's shoulder. Stopping beside her, he snorted softly. Marion rubbed him gently between the eyes.

Amy felt happy tears pricking at the back of her eyes. She knew that the moment had come — her mom had found a way to connect to this once frightened animal and in return had received its acceptance and trust.

As Marion sent Copper out again, Ty turned. "Come on, let's leave your mom to it," he said in a low voice. Amy nodded and quietly picked up her bag. They walked down past the turn-out fields, past the twelve-stall back barn and round to the front stable block.

Ty had started helping at Heartland three years ago, at first working at weekends and after school to earn money to help his family. Then at sixteen he had dropped out of high school to fulfil his ambition to work with horses full-time. Amy was glad. Ty had a great way with the horses and it was fun to have him around more.

"I have to groom Chester," said Ty, stopping to pick up a

halter and grooming bucket as they passed the tack-room.

Amy headed for the stall where a large bay hunter was looking out over his half-door. Chester had been staying at Heartland to overcome his fear of loading into horse trailers. "How are you, gorgeous?" she murmured, stroking him on the nose as Ty walked round with the halter.

"I didn't know you cared!" Ty grinned.

Amy hit him on the arm. "Like I meant you!"

Ty went into the stall and patted the big bay. "He's going home tomorrow. Your mom says he's ready."

"Tomorrow?" Amy said, her heart sinking slightly at the thought of saying goodbye. Having to say goodbye to the horses when they went to a new home or, as in Chester's case, returned to their owners, was one of the worst things about living and working at Heartland. "I'll miss him," she said softly.

Ty nodded. "Me too."

For a moment they both stood stroking Chester in silence.

"Hey, cheer up," Ty said. Amy realized he was looking at her downcast face. "At least it means…"

"That another horse can come and be helped," Amy finished off for him. She grinned as she saw the surprise on his face. "We were thinking the same thing."

"Gee, I need *help*!" Ty said. He dodged as she tried to hit him again.

"Do you know if Lou's rung?" she asked him, as he picked up a body brush and started to groom Chester.

Ty shook his head. "Nope. Why? Are you expecting her to call?"

Amy nodded eagerly. "Yeah. She's coming for my birthday. She said she'd call and say what time she's going to arrive." Amy's grey eyes shone at the thought of seeing her sister. "I can't wait to see her again. It's been ages!"

"And she's definitely coming?" Ty said questioningly.

"Yes." Amy saw his slightly sceptical expression. "*Yes!*" she insisted. "This time she's promised!"

Shouldering her bag, she let herself out of the stall and went down to the white-painted farmhouse that stood at a right angle to the stable block. She couldn't blame Ty for being doubtful. Ever since Lou had moved back from England to take up her high-powered banking job in New York a year ago, she had been promising to come and visit. So far, something had always seemed to come up at the last minute to prevent her.

Amy pushed open the back door and kicking off her trainers went into the kitchen. "Hi! I'm back!" she announced.

The kitchen was large but cluttered. In one corner there was a bookcase crammed to overflowing with books on horses and copies of horse magazines. The battered old table was littered with odds and ends – a hoofpick, a snaffle bit, one odd glove, a pot of keys.

Amy's grandfather, Jack Bartlett, was fixing a wooden grooming box at the kitchen table. "Hi, honey, how was your day?" he asked, putting down his screwdriver with a smile.

Amy rolled her eyes and fetched a Coke. "Better now school's over! Has Lou called?"

Jack Bartlett shook his head. "Not yet. I guess she'll call after work."

Amy nodded and took a couple of biscuits out of a jar. "I'm going to get changed, Grandpa."

She went up the winding stairs to her bedroom, taking them two at a time. As usual, her room was a mess. Dog-eared horse magazines littered the floor. The bed was unmade. Half a grooming kit was scattered on her bedroom table. As she pulled on her work jeans and a T-shirt she looked out at the front stable block. Chester was looking out over his door and Ty was going into Pegasus' stall. Amy scraped her long light brown hair into a scrunchie and hurried back down to the kitchen.

Just then the phone rang. "I'll get it," she said, as she grabbed the cordless phone off the side. "I bet it's Lou."

It was. "Telepathy," Amy exclaimed. "I knew it was you."

"Yes, it's me," said Lou. "Hi."

"What time are you coming tomorrow?" Amy asked, eagerly. "We're having dinner at seven o'clock but Mom said you'd probably come earlier. I can't wait to see you!"

"Well…"

Amy heard the hesitation in her sister's voice. "You *are* still coming, aren't you?" she demanded.

"I'm sorry, Amy," Lou said awkwardly. "But something's come up at work … I just can't put it off."

"But you promised!" Amy protested. "And it's my birthday!" She knew she sounded like a six-year-old, but she didn't care. She couldn't believe that Lou was cancelling again.

"I know it is and I'm sorry. I really am." Lou's voice suddenly brightened, "Look, why don't you come and visit me here again? We can go shopping or go to a show. Do whatever you like."

"Yeah, sure," Amy said, flatly.

"Can you tell Mom and Grandpa I'm sorry?" Lou said. "I've sent you something in the post. And Carl sends his love."

Amy didn't say anything. Carl Anderson was Lou's boyfriend. Amy had met him only once and she hadn't liked him. When she had told him about their mother's work he had laughed, "Horse shrinks, what will they think of next?" She didn't know what Lou saw in him.

Lou seemed to feel the uncomfortable pause. "We'll catch up soon," she said quickly. "Promise. But I must go now. Bye!"

Amy put the phone down with a bang. She should have known! She met Grandpa's eyes. He looked at her in concern. "Isn't Lou coming?" he asked.

"No!" Amy said angrily. "She has work to do. *As usual!*"

Jack Bartlett sighed. "You know what Lou's like about her job, honey — it's very important to her."

"My fifteenth birthday's important, too!" Amy exclaimed.

"And anyway, it was just an excuse. She just doesn't want to come here! You know she doesn't! She makes an excuse every time."

Grandpa didn't deny it. "She finds it difficult," he said with a sigh. "You know she does."

Amy scowled and threw herself down in a chair. Grandpa squeezed her shoulder and disappeared into the hall. "Here's something that might cheer you up," he said, coming back in and handing her a new copy of *Horse Life*.

"It's come!" Amy exclaimed, temporarily forgetting about her sister and sitting up. She opened the magazine and scanned down the contents page. Yes! There it was — LIFE AT HEARTLAND, page twenty-three.

She flicked through. What did the article say about them?

> *In the rolling hills of North-Eastern Virginia, Marion Fleming, "the horse lady", works her magic at Heartland, a rescue home for horses, ponies and donkeys, based at Heartland Farm. Horses come here to be healed and to have the scars of the past taken away.*

Amy grinned. She liked that line. She read on:

> *Marion Fleming, once one of the world's finest female showjumpers, started Heartland following the break-up of her marriage twelve years ago. A fall at the Show-Jumping World Championships left her then husband, British show-*

jumper Tim Fleming, in a wheelchair and unable to ride again.

Frowning, Amy quickly read over the rest of the paragraph. It was about her father's accident. About how, as favourite to win the gold medal, he had been racing against the clock and had brought his horse, Pegasus, in too sharply to the last fence. Unable to take off properly, Pegasus had caught the top pole of the jump between his legs and come crashing down, landing on his rider. Tim Fleming had been temporarily paralysed in the fall.

Uncomfortable feelings prickled through Amy. She had only been three at the time and didn't have any clear memories of the accident or the aftermath when Daddy – unable to cope with his injuries – had abandoned them. Her first real memories were of Heartland, her grandpa's home, where she and her mom had eventually come to live with Pegasus. Her eyes skipped over the words in front of her. It was a relief to find that the next paragraph focused on Heartland again:

> *With its eighteen stables, Heartland is a recovery centre for horses that have been rescued from dreadful neglect or physical cruelty. Horses who have been deemed dangerous and unrideable or who have nowhere else to go and no one else who can help. Using a mixture of conventional veterinary medicine and other treatments learnt while*

11

nursing the great Pegasus back to physical and mental health, Marion Fleming finds ways to reach these horses. When they get better, concerted efforts are made to find each of them a new and permanent home.

The article went on to explain that Marion also treated privately owned horses with behavioural problems. Amy raced through to the end.

"What's it like?" Jack Bartlett asked when she looked up.

"Great!" Amy enthused, her bad mood forgotten. "It makes Mom sound totally amazing. We'll have loads of people who want to bring their horses here!" She jumped to her feet.

"Now, Amy, don't go counting your chickens..."

But Amy shrugged off his practical words. Excitement bubbled through her. "Has Mom seen it?" she asked eagerly.

"Not yet," Grandpa replied.

"I've got to show her!" Amy said.

She pulled on her trainers and raced up the yard, hoping that her mom would have finished with Copper by now. Her mind was buzzing with ideas. The article was bound to bring them lots more paying clients and that meant more money, which meant they could afford to help more horses. Her imagination took over. She saw a new twenty-stall barn and another horse trailer and pick-up. Maybe even an indoor ring for the winter when the outdoor riding rings were often hock-deep in mud. Her biggest ambition was for

Heartland to be as successful as possible. This could just be the way for that to happen!

She reached the ring. Her mom was standing in the middle, patting Copper. "Come on in," she called to Amy.

Amy climbed over the gate. "The article that *Horse Life* did on us has come out! Look!" she said, hurrying over.

Marion took the magazine from her and began reading the article while Amy carefully stroked Copper's warm neck.

"I like this line," Marion laughed. "Healing the scars — that's good."

"Me too!" grinned Amy. She fed Copper a mint from her pocket. He snuffled it up, his warm breath grazing her palm. "You're a good boy," she told him, very gently rubbing his face.

Marion smiled, momentarily distracted from the magazine. "You couldn't have done that to him four weeks ago."

Amy nodded and looked over her mother's shoulder. "Isn't the article good? I bet lots of people will want to bring their horses here for us to help. Heartland will get loads of money."

"We're not doing too badly at the moment as it is," Marion pointed out. "We've got almost more paying clients than we can deal with." Since she had started Heartland, Marion's reputation had grown. They were now getting a steady stream of owners who hoped she might cure their horses of behavioural problems.

"But if we get *even more* then we can build a new barn and help loads more rescue horses," said Amy.

Marion smiled. "Let's wait and see what happens." She handed back the magazine to Amy. "Come on, let's take this boy in."

They led Copper through the gate and down the yard. As they reached his stall, Amy suddenly remembered her other, less good, news. "Lou called," she said. "She's not coming."

"Oh," Marion said, her face falling.

Amy told her about the phone call. "It's the same as always," she said, quick anger rising inside her again. "She never comes. She says she will and then she doesn't. She doesn't care about *us*, all she cares about is her stupid job and Carl!"

"Amy, you know that's not true," said Marion, picking up a body brush and starting to brush Copper over. "Lou loves you, loves all of us. She just finds it difficult coming here."

"But that's so crazy!" Amy exclaimed. "This is her *home*!"

"No it isn't, Amy," Marion said. "You know it isn't."

Amy wanted to resist what her mom was saying, but deep down she knew it was true.

After Daddy had left, Lou had refused to move to Virginia. Convinced that her father would one day come back, she had begged to be allowed to stay on at her English boarding school. Marion had agreed because she couldn't bear to put Lou through any more emotional stress. Instead of spending school holidays at Heartland, Lou had nearly always found an excuse to stay with friends in England. When she had come over, she'd made no secret of the fact that she blamed horses for Daddy's accident and sudden departure, and that she felt Marion and Amy had been wrong to leave England.

With her English accent it was sometimes hard to believe she was American at all – let alone Amy's sister.

Amy sighed. Despite their differences, they were still sisters. "I just want to see her, Mom."

"I know you do, honey," Marion said sympathetically. "And you will. She'll come back one day."

"Yeah, maybe when I'm sixty!" Amy retorted. "Why can't she just forget about Daddy's accident? It happened so long ago."

Marion shook her head. "I know it seems like that to you," she said. "But Lou was older and she was really close to Daddy. They were inseparable." She half smiled. "He was so proud of her when she was little. He used to put her on all our horses, and she would ride anything. She's a lot like him – brave and practical. You know, Lou was amazing after his accident." She sighed and Amy saw the sadness in her eyes. "She was so strong and took charge of so many things. I don't really know how we would have managed without her."

Marion looked down and there was a pause. Amy swallowed, suddenly feeling a pang of guilt. She never thought about how much her mom must miss Lou too.

Marion stroked Copper's forelock and then forced a smile. "Lou will come to terms with it all in the end," she said to Amy. "You'll see." Giving Copper a final pat, she walked out of the stall. In the next stall along, Pegasus was looking out. He whickered a soft welcome, his dark eyes lighting up as Marion walked along to greet him. She placed a hand lovingly against his great, grey head.

Amy followed her. "Am I like Daddy, too?"

For a moment, Marion didn't answer.

"Mom?" Amy persisted. The older Amy got, the more she found herself wondering about her father but her mom rarely wanted to talk about him.

Marion looked at Amy's tall, slim frame, her brown hair and thickly-lashed grey eyes. "On the outside, yes, you look like him," she said quietly. "But inside I think you're a lot more like me – emotional, intuitive." She smiled. "I guess that's why we make such a great team. Lou – now she's practical, feet firmly on the ground."

"Like Daddy?" Amy said.

"Yes," Marion said, nodding. She stopped, her eyes darkening with pain, and she looked down. "Well … like I always *thought* he was," she whispered, her voice so quiet that Amy hardly caught the words. She didn't say anything for a long moment. Then she looked into Amy's worried face and seemed to force herself to smile. "Come on, don't look like that," she said. "Hey, I tell you what, why don't you take one of the ponies out for a ride when we've fed the horses? It's such a perfect afternoon. Ty and I can finish off the work."

Amy was surprised by her mother's offer. It was rare she

got to go out trail riding on school days – riding for pleasure always came second to getting the work done. "OK," she said, brightening up.

Marion smiled. "It is almost your birthday, after all."

"Soraya's coming round later," Amy said. "I'll see if she wants to come." Soraya Martin had been her best friend since third grade and she loved horses almost as much as Amy did.

Marion nodded. "Good idea. You two go and enjoy yourselves."

Just then the back door opened and Jack Bartlett looked out. "Marion! Telephone!" he called.

With a quick smile at Amy, Marion hurried off down the yard. Amy moved closer to Pegasus. He nuzzled her and she leant her head against his comfortingly strong neck. As far as she was concerned, loving and caring for Pegasus seemed to bring Daddy closer. She wished Lou could feel the same way. "When do you think Lou will come home?" she said to him. Pegasus snorted quietly in reply. Amy hugged him. At least he was always there for her to talk to. "I love you," she whispered.

As she waited for her mom, she let her fingers work on his ears with light, circular movements that helped release tension, fear and pain. It was one of the many alternative treatments that Marion used on the horses that came to Heartland. In response to Amy's skilful fingers Pegasus lowered his enormous head, obviously enjoying the attention.

A few minutes later, Marion came back out of the house. "That was Wayne Taylor," she said, "wanting to make arrangements for picking up Chester tomorrow morning." Two of the horses further along the stable block, Jake and Tarka, kicked impatiently at their doors. Marion smiled. "Come on," she said, "let's go and feed these horses."

In the feed-room, the sweet smell of beet pulp filled the air. Cobwebs hung off the beamed ceiling and the floor was made of old, cracked flagstones. Marion started scooping bran, barley and alfalfa cubes into the battered yellow feeding buckets. "When you're out would you ride up to Mrs Bell's for me?" she asked. "I promised her I'd drop in some herbs to help with Sugarfoot's sweet-itch."

"Sure," Amy said. Mrs Bell was an old lady who lived in a tiny house up a lonely track. She owned a little Shetland pony called Sugarfoot. He followed her everywhere, more like a dog than a pony. Amy sometimes dropped by to give Mrs Bell a hand looking after him. "Then after we've seen Mrs Bell, we can go on over to Clairdale Ridge," she said, starting to add a scoopful of the soaked beet pulp to each bucket. "Soraya hasn't seen the Mallens' new horse yet."

Her mom frowned. "Grandpa heard a rumour in town that the Mallens were moving."

"Already?" Amy said, surprised. "They haven't been there that long." The Mallen family were the tenants of a dilapidated old house on Clairdale Ridge. They had a clutch of skinny animals – hens, dogs, and a couple of cows. Just recently, a beautiful young bay stallion had joined the cattle in the sparse field at the front of the house, and Amy had ridden past to admire him whenever she could. "Where are they moving to?" she asked.

"No one seems to know," said Marion, picking up the dusty cod-liver oil can and adding a dollop to each feed. "Hopefully somewhere with better grazing for those poor animals. But it might just be a rumour that they're going."

"I'll check it out," Amy said.

Marion looked at her warningly. "Don't forget to stick to the trails. That road up to Clairdale Ridge is far too dangerous to ride on."

"OK, Mom," Amy sighed. Her mom had warned her about that road about a thousand times. Shaking her head, she picked up a pile of feeds and set off for the front stable block.

Chapter Two

After finishing the feeding, Amy went down to the ponies' field. A pretty black pony standing by the gate whickered a greeting. "Hi, Jaz," Amy said, pulling a packet of mints out of her pocket and offering one to the mare. Jasmine gobbled it down greedily, her soft muzzle immediately nudging at Amy, asking for more.

Alerted by the rustle of the paper the other ponies in the field looked up, ears pricked. They crowded over to the gate and Amy began distributing the mints between them as fairly as she could. Suddenly the little group scattered as a buckskin pony came barging through, ears back, teeth snapping.

"Sundance!" Amy exclaimed as the buckskin stopped dead and thrust his head hard against her chest. He rolled his eyes threateningly at the other ponies, warning them to keep back. "You're a bully!" she told him severely.

Sundance looked up adoringly at her. *Who, me?* he seemed to say as he nuzzled her and snorted happily. Amy kissed his golden head. Sundance looked up at her cutely and then spoiled the impression by kicking out at Jasmine who was edging past him. Amy sighed. Nothing was ever going to change Sundance's bad temper but she didn't mind, she loved him anyway.

She had fallen in love with him the first moment she saw him in a pen at a horse sale two years ago. With his small ears back and his head high, he had defied the world, attacking anyone who dared to try and enter his pen to inspect him. "He'll go for meat," Amy heard two men say. But he hadn't. Amy had persuaded her mom to buy him and had worked with him, slowly gaining his trust and affection. Much to everyone's surprise, Sundance had proved to have an exceptional talent for jumping. Now there were lots of people who wanted him. But Marion had promised Amy that he would never be sold.

"Amy!"

Amy turned. Soraya was running up the track with a halter in her hands, her black curls bouncing on her shoulders.

"Hi!" Amy called.

"Hi there!" Soraya panted. "I just got here. Your mom said we can go out for a trail ride."

Amy nodded. "Who do you want? I'm going to ride Sundance."

Soraya only had to think for a second. "I'll ride Jasmine."

She knew the horses and ponies at Heartland almost as well as Amy did.

Jasmine was another long-term resident at Heartland. An ex-dressage pony, she had been about to be put to sleep because she was lame on her front legs owing to soft swellings around her fetlocks; then Marion had rescued her. And now, after successful treatment to her windgalls, Jasmine was sound enough for light work. She was a pretty pony, half-Arabian with a dished face, a white star and two white socks. In contrast to Sundance she had the sweetest of natures and loved everyone. Although it would be hard to part with her, Amy hoped that one day she'd find a new home.

It didn't take Amy and Soraya long to bring the ponies in from the field then groom and tack them up. Before setting off, Amy picked up the herbs for Sugarfoot from her mom and put them in her saddlebag.

They rode on to the sandy trail that led up Teak's Hill, the wooded slope that rose steeply behind Heartland. As they headed towards Mrs Bell's house, the trees on the slope cast a welcome shade.

"So, do you know when Lou's coming, yet?" Soraya asked.

"She's not," Amy replied. "She called and cancelled."

"What – again?" Soraya said.

"Yes, again."

Soraya looked at her sympathetically and then, sensitive as always, she changed the subject. "What do you think you'll get for your birthday?"

"Well," Amy replied enthusiastically, deciding not to think about Lou any more. "I want that blue jacket in the window of Cooper's — you know, the waterproof one. I've shown it to Mom about ten times now."

"Oh, yeah," Soraya nodded. Cooper's was the local saddlers. They visited it every time they went into town.

"And some new gloves and show breeches," Amy continued.

Soraya smiled. "Do you think Matt will get you a gift?"

Amy thought about Matt Trewin, tall with sandy hair, brown eyes and a lopsided grin. She shrugged. "I don't know."

"I bet he will!" Soraya said. "It's so totally obvious he likes you. He's always hanging round with you at school or coming up to visit Heartland..."

"That's because he comes up with Scott," Amy interrupted. "Not to see me." Matt's older brother Scott was the local equine vet, and often when he visited Heartland Matt would be in the car with him and would get out and hang round with Amy. "He says he wants to find out about being a vet."

"Like that's true!" Soraya said, rolling her eyes. "Everyone *knows* Matt wants to be a doctor."

"Well ... maybe he's thinking about changing his mind," Amy said.

"Amy!" Soraya exclaimed. "Quit acting dumb! You *know* Matt wants to date you. Why don't you just admit it and say yes? I would!"

Amy struggled to find the words. It wasn't that she didn't like Matt, he was fun to be around and they got on just fine, it was just... "I wish he liked riding more," she said. "He's not exactly into horses, is he? Not like Scott," she added, thinking about twenty-nine-year-old Scott who was devoted to horses. She saw Soraya's incredulous expression.

"Amy!" Soraya cried. "I don't get you sometimes! The cutest boy in school totally adores you and all you can think about is that he isn't really into horses. Nearly every girl in our class would give anything to be going out with Matt! He's good-looking, intelligent, caring. I wish I could meet someone half as nice. I only ever get to go out with jerks!" The last boy Soraya had been out with had two-timed her. Her face brightened. "Still, who knows, maybe I'll meet someone at camp."

"I bet you will!" Amy said.

At the beginning of July, Soraya was going off to a riding camp for a month. It was a camp where you got to look after one horse all the time and enter in competitions. Soraya's parents had organized it for her as a special treat. Amy thought about having a whole month without her best friend. "I'll miss you," she said wistfully.

"Sure," Soraya stroked Jasmine's neck. "And I'll miss you too — and all the horses. But I'll be back in August."

Amy grinned at her. "With a new boyfriend, maybe."

Soraya's face lit up. "I hope!"

They giggled and pushed the ponies into a canter. It was

cool in the shade of the trees and as they rode along side by side, the wind rushing by, Amy felt she could have gone on forever. However, they soon reached the dirt track that led to Mrs Bell's small clapboard house with its ramshackle fence.

"Whoa, boy." Amy eased Sundance to a halt. "I wonder where Mrs Bell is," she said to Soraya.

Just then, Jasmine neighed and an answering whinny came from down the side of the house. Amy and Soraya looked at each other, dismounted and then led the ponies round the back to the garden, where they saw Mrs Bell kneeling in the sparse vegetable patch. She was slowly digging up carrots and putting them in a basket next to her on the ground. Each carrot seemed to take enormous effort. Beside her stood a tiny Shetland pony. As Mrs Bell worked she sang in a cracked, quavering voice.

"Hello, Mrs Bell," Amy called out, but the old lady didn't hear. She continued singing. Sugarfoot stood happily beside her, his ears pricked.

"Let's leave Sundance and Jasmine here," Amy said to Soraya. They hitched the ponies to a fence post and then went up the path to the vegetable patch.

Every time Mrs Bell finished digging an area of soil, she moved further along the row of carrots and Sugarfoot, the little pony, followed her. Mrs Bell was wearing a torn apron and an old hat but Sugarfoot looked in excellent condition. His chestnut coat gleamed. His blond mane and tail were free of tangles and from underneath his bushy forelock, his eyes peeped out, dark and bright.

Mrs Bell turned to pat the little Shetland and murmured, "What do you think, Sugarfoot – the pumpkins aren't doing so good this summer, are they?"

Sugarfoot pushed against her hand and whickered softly.

"He is *so* cute!" Soraya said.

"Mrs Bell," Amy called again.

The old lady started in surprise at her voice and then, seeing it was Amy and Soraya, a smile lit up her face. "Hello there," she said, straightening up slowly and smiling broadly. "How nice to see you both." Sugarfoot trotted over to Soraya and nuzzled against her, searching for a treat. "Would you girls like a drink?" Mrs Bell asked them.

"I'm OK, thanks," said Amy, looking at Soraya who also shook her head. "We just came to see how you were and to give you some herbs for Sugarfoot. Mom said they're for his sweet-itch. How are you, Mrs Bell?"

"Oh, me, I'm fine and dandy."

Amy didn't think Mrs Bell looked fine at all. The old lady was breathing heavily with a strange wheezing sound.

"Do you want a hand?" Soraya offered.

"That's kind of you, honey. If you could carry the basket indoors for me that would be a big help."

The girls followed Mrs Bell into the house, Soraya carrying the vegetable basket and Amy bringing the packet of herbs. Mrs Bell leant against Sugarfoot's neck for support.

Amy was amazed at how the little pony seemed to understand exactly how to help his owner. He came right into the kitchen, letting the old lady support herself on him until she was able to sink down into a chair.

Amy looked round at the ancient, cracked sink, the single chair at the table and the threadbare blue rug on the wooden boards, and breathed in the stale air that smelt of boiled vegetables. Sugarfoot helped himself to an apple from the fruit bowl that stood on a low table beside the door.

"Is he allowed to do that?" Soraya asked, surprised.

"Oh, he only ever takes one," said Mrs Bell. She stroked Sugarfoot's neck and he slobbered apple appreciatively on to her apron and then rested his head against her shoulder. "And he knows he's only allowed in the kitchen," she continued, adding, "He's what makes this place home for me."

"How long have you had him?" asked Soraya, who didn't know Mrs Bell as well as Amy.

"Twelve years. I still remember that first day I saw him." Mrs Bell shook her head fondly at the memory. "Just weaned, he was, and the tiniest foal ever. I *had* to buy him. He's been with me ever since." Sugarfoot nuzzled her shoulder and Mrs Bell put a hand on his neck. "Well, better get on," she said. "There's the housework to do."

"Are you sure you're OK, Mrs Bell?" said Amy, concerned. She always felt worried about the old lady, all alone up on Teak's Hill. No one ever seemed to visit her apart from Eric Beasley, the postman, and Amy herself.

Mrs Bell smiled at her. "Of course I'm OK, honey. I've got Sugarfoot to look after me."

As they rode back down the hill, Amy turned to Soraya. "I think we should go and see Mrs Bell more often."

Soraya nodded in agreement. "She sure doesn't look too well, does she?"

Amy shook her head. "I'll tell Mom when we get back." She looked across Teak's Hill. Clairdale Ridge rose up, dark and craggy against the blue sky. The sun was still beating down on them but in the distance, near the ridge, a group of dark clouds seemed to be gathering. "Shall we go over to the Mallens' house?" she said.

Soraya grinned. "Yeah! I want to see this horse you keep talking about."

"He's gorgeous!" Amy said.

The track widened out and they pushed the ponies into a canter. Amy leant forward. Seeing two fallen tree trunks lying to one side, she steered towards them and kicked Sundance on. As always at the sight of a jump, his ears pricked up, his head rose and his stride became full of energy. As he reached the logs, Amy felt his muscles bunch and gather. He cleared the jump by at least half a metre and threw in a buck for good measure as he landed. Grabbing his mane, Amy laughed.

They slowed down. "He's jumping well!" Soraya said, patting Jasmine's black neck. "Are you taking him to any shows over the summer?"

Amy nodded. Sundance was a natural in the Large Pony Hunter classes. With Amy riding him he seemed to sparkle in front of an audience, meeting each jump perfectly, never touching a pole and jumping with such athletic ability and style that judges could rarely resist him. In the ring he was a picture of good manners and obedience. It was just lucky the judges never saw him at home, Amy thought dryly, as he swung his head grumpily at Jasmine, his ears pinned back.

Soraya grinned. "Ashley'd better watch out."

They both giggled. Ashley Grant was at school with them. Beautiful and wealthy, she was also a talented rider. Her parents owned a smart livery stable called Green Briar where her mom, Val Grant, was the trainer. Ashley rode in all of the shows and had won lots of prizes with her expensive push-button ponies. When she had first seen Amy arrive at a show with Sundance, she had christened him The Mule because of his unfavourable buckskin coat and displays of bad temper outside the ring. She had laughed less, however, when Sundance cantered into the ring, ears perfectly pricked, and had won the blue ribbon.

"Did I tell you that Ashley's mom wanted to buy Sundance?" she said.

"You're kidding!" Soraya replied, surprised.

"She rang last week." Amy grinned. "She offered loads of money. Mom said no, of course." She patted Sundance's neck. "As if I'd ever let you go somewhere like Green Briar!"

Green Briar's training methods were very different from those used at Heartland. Val Grant believed in force and very firm discipline. She schooled ponies to respond to the commands of any rider – her horses learnt to excel in one area and would complete a course to win. Val Grant considered it a waste of time developing relationships with them. It made Amy angry that anyone could treat horses with anything less than the respect and understanding they deserved.

At that moment, Jasmine stepped too close to Sundance. He squealed and snapped his teeth. "On second thoughts," Amy said, shaking her head, "maybe Ashley's welcome to you!" She laughed and patted Sundance quickly to show that she didn't mean it.

She wondered how many shows they would get to that summer. She had a secret ambition to try him in Junior Jumpers as well as doing the Pony Hunter classes. The problem was finding the time. If Heartland was busy then Mom couldn't take her. But she didn't really mind. As much as she liked competing, it wasn't the most important thing in her life – *that* was helping out with the horses at Heartland.

"Let's trot," Soraya said. Amy nodded.

The nearer they got to Clairdale Ridge, the rougher the terrain became. The steep sides of the mountain were covered with tufted grass and rocky outcroppings. A few lonely buildings huddled on its slopes.

They reached the trail that led up past the Mallens' house.

"Look!" Amy said, halting Sundance. Three strands of barbed wire were attached to posts on opposite sides of the trail. They were at chest height to the ponies and too dangerous to jump. Anyhow, Amy thought, the trails were usually only blocked if they were impassable.

"Maybe there's been a rock-slide or something," Soraya said, stopping Jasmine beside Sundance. She looked up – the black clouds that had been in the far distance were getting closer now. "Maybe we should just go back. The weather's not looking so good."

"But we're so close!" Amy protested. She was keen to see the bay stallion again. "We can take the road instead."

"But your mom's always telling us not to use that road," Soraya said doubtfully.

"It'll be OK." The thought of the stallion drove Amy on. "We'll only be on it for five minutes. Come on!" She urged Sundance forward. Looking back over her shoulder she saw her friend hesitate for a moment before following.

The road was narrow and winding and on either side there were crumbling stone walls topped with old wooden posts and rusty barbed wire.

"It doesn't look too safe," Soraya said, looking ahead at the sharp bends.

"Look, it'll be OK," repeated Amy impatiently.

They trotted up the road, the ponies' hooves clattering loudly on the worn asphalt. As they came around the second bend the road plunged into a dark tunnel of trees. Sundance snorted uncertainly and stopped.

"It's all right," Amy urged him. "Walk on."

Sundance stepped forward into the darkness, high-footed and cautious. The air felt suddenly cold, the leafy canopy overhead blocking out the warmth of the sun.

With a wild squawk, a jay suddenly flew out of a nearby tree. Both Jasmine and Sundance shied violently, losing their footing on the smooth surface. Amy glanced back at Soraya. Her face was tense.

"Let's trot again," Amy said quickly. She was beginning to have the uncomfortable feeling that her mom was right. This *was* a dangerous road to ride on. It would take just one car to come round the corner too fast...

Clicking her tongue, she pushed Sundance on. He was agitated and skittish, but she soothed him and he settled into a steady trot. Amy was glad when a couple of minutes later they emerged from the tunnel of trees. Ahead of them was the track that led to the Mallens' house. She turned down it in relief.

As they drew closer to the house, Amy frowned and slowed Sundance to a walk. "They've gone!" she said in surprise.

The house was undoubtedly empty. The bay horse and the scrawny cows were missing from the field, the rusty pick-up had disappeared, and the windows were bare and curtain-less. Only a few bags of rubbish by the door suggested that there had been people living there recently.

"Oh." Soraya sounded disappointed.

Amy's heart sank. She had really wanted to see the stallion again. "I guess we should go home then," she said despondently.

They rode around the side of the house, heading for a trail that led off the track back to Teak's Hill and Heartland. They passed a collection of dilapidated wooden outbuildings. The air had become heavy and still, dark clouds pressing down overhead.

"This is spooky," Soraya said in a low voice.

Suddenly Jasmine put her head in the air and whinnied shrilly. Both girls jumped. "Jaz!" Amy exclaimed. The words died on her lips as an answering whinny echoed through the still air. She and Soraya stared at each other in shock.

"Where did that come from?" Soraya gasped.

"I-I don't know!" Amy stammered. She looked round wildly, almost believing that she must have heard a ghost. And then a second whinny came.

This time Amy caught the direction it was coming from. "That barn!" she said, pointing to one of the sturdier looking outbuildings. She grabbed her reins as Sundance side-stepped, his head up and his cream ears pricked. Soraya was struggling with Jasmine, who was whinnying excitedly again. Amy dismounted quickly and led Sundance over to Soraya, thrusting his reins at her. "Here, hold him!"

As she ran the short distance over to the shed, a large raindrop splashed down on to her arm. She ignored it, her fingers fumbling with the door's rusty metal bolt. She could hear a hoof pawing at the floor on the other side. Why was a horse shut in this barn? What sort of condition would it be in? The bolt jerked back but the door was stiff and heavy and stayed in place.

"Be careful!" Soraya called anxiously.

Amy had been about to throw all her weight into heaving the door open but she checked herself. Soraya was right – the horse would be terrified by being shut in the dark, and fear made any horse dangerous.

Amy cautiously edged the door open a crack and peered in. For a moment she couldn't see anything but then her eyes gradually adjusted to the dim light. She gasped.

At the back of the stall, eyeing her suspiciously, was the Mallens' beautiful bay horse.

Chapter Three

"It's the stallion!" Amy called, motioning frantically to Soraya. She tugged the door further open, bumping it heavily along the ground. Once the door was open far enough to let in some light, she could see the stallion clearly – and he could see her. His eyes rolled in fear as he stood at the back of the barn, his muscles bunched and tense, his shoulders and flanks quivering.

"It's OK," Amy said to him as soothingly as she could. "I won't hurt you." Her eyes swept round the shed. The floor was bare and there was no water or food. However, the stallion's physical condition was good which meant he couldn't have been shut in for more than a day or two.

The horse called out shrilly. Amy's mind raced. If she opened the door further he might try and break free. That could be disastrous – he would either escape on to the wilds of Clairdale Ridge or end up on the narrow road. But they had to help him somehow. She swung round to Soraya. "We've got to do something!"

Soraya had her own problems. Excited by the stallion's whinnies, Sundance and Jasmine were whirling round. Sundance tried to bite Jasmine, causing the mare to rear backwards. Soraya only just managed to keep her seat.

Amy looked up at the dark sky. It had begun to rain heavily. Large drops were splashing down. Her heart pounding, she turned again to the barn and started squeezing through the gap in the door.

"Easy, now," she called to the frightened stallion. He half reared and she jumped back. "Steady!" But the horse wouldn't be calmed. He kicked out, his back hooves crashing against the barn wall.

"Amy!" Soraya called from outside. "I can't hold on to Sundance much longer!"

Amy hesitated. She knew Soraya needed help, but what about the horse? The rain was pelting down now, bouncing off the roof and forming puddles on the ground. Her mind was in a whirl. Even if she could get near the stallion how was she going to get him back to Heartland without a halter or bridle?

"Amy!" Soraya's voice was higher, more desperate, now.

Amy made up her mind. She squeezed back out of the shed and dragged the door shut. "I'm sorry!" she whispered through the crack, as she rammed the bolts home. "But I'll be back soon."

The stallion cried out frantically as he found himself in the dark again. Trying to shut out the sound, Amy turned away. Sundance had reared up and Soraya was struggling to hold on to him.

Amy raced over to her friend. She grabbed his reins and pulled him down. "Quick! We've got to get help!" Steadying Sundance, Amy swung herself up into the saddle and the two girls set off down the trail at a gallop.

By the time they got back to Heartland Amy and Soraya were soaked to the skin, their jodhpurs clinging to their legs and their T-shirts plastered against their bodies.

They clattered into the yard at a tremendous pace that brought Marion Fleming hurrying out of the tack-room. "What on earth are you doing?" She looked at Amy's wide eyes and pale face and her tone changed. "What's happened?" she asked anxiously.

"The Mallens' horse!" Amy gasped, sliding off Sundance. "They've gone, but it's shut up in a barn outside their house. Mom! You've got to help!"

"It's been abandoned?" Marion said.

Amy nodded. "We've got to go and get it!"

Marion looked at the rain pouring down around them. "We can't take the trailer out in this, Amy! The roads up on Clairdale Ridge are so steep and narrow. It would be too dangerous."

Amy pushed away the picture of the forbidding tunnel of

trees high up on the ridge. "But we can't leave that horse shut in for another night!" she cried. "It hasn't got food or water or anything!"

"Nothing?" Marion said quickly.

Amy shook her head. "It's terrified, Mom! If a storm starts it might try and break free!"

Marion made up her mind. "OK, we'll go get it," she said decisively. Her voice became brisk and efficient. "You put the ponies away and get a bucket of food for the stallion. I'll get the trailer out." She hurried off. "See you in a minute."

"Here!" Soraya said, reaching to take Sundance's reins off Amy. "Go now. I'll put Sundance and Jasmine away. I'd better not come with you. Dad will be here to pick me up soon." Amy hesitated for a moment. "Go on!" Soraya urged. "You can call me tonight and tell me what happens."

"OK! Thanks!" Amy gasped. Turning, she ran after her mom.

As they drove out of Heartland the weather seemed to get even worse. The sky was heavy and dark grey. The windscreen wipers squeaked rhythmically back and forth, barely making a break in the sheeting rain. The tyres splashed noisily through the water on the road.

Amy shivered in her damp clothes. "Why do you think the Mallens left him, Mom?"

Marion shook her head, her eyes glued to the road. "I guess he might have been stolen, and then before they'd found someone to sell him off to they got scared. Maybe the police had been asking around."

"I can't believe they could just abandon him like that!" Amy exclaimed. "He could have starved to death."

Marion looked grim as she turned the trailer up the steep, winding road that led up Clairdale Ridge. "People like the Mallens don't care about things like that." The gearbox clunked as she changed down a gear to negotiate the sharp bends. Water was running in streams down the road.

They headed into the gloomy tunnel of trees. The truck and trailer crawled round the tight bends. A branch cracked loudly and thudded on to the roof. Amy jumped. She didn't like this dark passageway one bit. A tree creaked alarmingly as they passed. Amy gripped the seat and concentrated on rescuing the horse.

At last they emerged into the open. "I can hardly see a thing," Marion said, as heavy rain hit the windscreen again.

Amy peered through the blur, searching the track that led up to the farmhouse. "There! There's the turn. Not far now, Mom."

The truck splashed along the rutted driveway. Marion stopped it outside the house and jumped out, leaving the headlights on to illuminate their way. Amy grabbed the halter and lead-rope from the seat beside her while Marion put the trailer ramp down. "Which building is it?" she called to Amy.

"That one!" Amy shouted, raising her voice above the wind.

They staggered through the rain to the barn. After Marion had pulled back the bolts, they heaved the door open together so it stood slightly ajar. Amy looked in. The bay stallion stared at them, head up, nostrils flaring, eyes wild. Marion looked at him for a moment and then turned her back to the wind and took out a small container from her pocket. From inside, she took a pinch of dark, gritty dust and rubbed it into her hands. "Stand back a bit," she said softly to Amy.

Amy did as she was told and Marion squeezed through the gap in the door. The horse moved uneasily on the spot, his ears back. Turning herself sideways on to him, Marion looked at the floor. The stallion regarded her warily. Very slowly she held out her hand. The bay made to jerk his head back but then he seemed to suddenly catch the scent of the powder. His nostrils flared and he inhaled, his ears suddenly pricking up.

Amy held her breath. The powder was made from chestnut trimmings which were insensitive, horny growths found on the inside of horses' front legs. An old horseman had once taught Marion that the scent would calm nervous and frightened horses. Now, sheltering in the doorway, Amy watched to see what would happen.

Very cautiously, the horse stretched out his head. Marion stayed absolutely still, eyes averted. *I am no threat*, her body language seemed to be saying. The horse took a step forward, all the time breathing in. His delicate muzzle touched

Marion's hand, his nostrils dilating. He took another step forward and lifted his head to her hair, breathing in and then out.

Very slowly, Amy saw her mom turn, and as the stallion breathed in again the fear left his eyes. His muscles relaxed and he lowered his head to nuzzle Marion's hand. She stroked him. "Pass me the halter," she said quietly to Amy.

Without the slightest objection, the horse let Marion slip on the halter. She patted him. "Come on, boy, let's get you into the trailer."

Amy heaved the door open. The horse obediently followed Marion out into the sheeting rain. Amy patted him and he nuzzled her arm. Now his initial fear was gone he seemed friendly, even affectionate.

When they reached the trailer she stood on the ramp and rattled a feed bucket. The horse stretched out his head and neck and gobbled a mouthful. Then, with no more prompting, he walked calmly into the box. Amy put down the bucket to let him eat and then, leaving her mom to tie him up, she slipped out of the side door to pull up the ramp. Her wet fingers slipped as she fastened the bolts. The wind and rain lashed down. At last Marion emerged. "Home," she said, coming round to check the bolts. "And fast."

Their faces were streaming with water as they climbed back into the truck. Marion turned the key and the engine spluttered into life. Amy shivered and squeezed water from her hair. Marion turned on the heater. It roared noisily, competing with the sound of the rain. They could hear the stallion move uneasily in the back as the rain battered the roof of the trailer.

Outside there was an ominous rumbling. Seconds later, a jagged fork of lightning split the sky and the rain started to sheet down with a new intensity. As they turned on to the steep road downwards, a crash of thunder broke over them.

The horse began to panic. His feet thudded against the side of the box, causing it to rock alarmingly. Amy glanced anxiously at her mother. The truck was gathering speed as it headed down the hill. Marion was concentrating hard, braking slowly and steadily to keep the trailer under control on the wet road.

"This is insane," muttered Marion. "I should never have let you talk me into this, Amy." Her eyes showed her anxiety as she gripped the steering wheel tightly.

Amy jumped as lightning forked straight down through the sky accompanied by an immense clap of thunder. The stallion's hooves crashed into the walls of the trailer again and again as he struggled to escape from his moving prison.

The tunnel of dark trees loomed up ahead. As they entered, branches closed over the top of the trailer, banging and scraping against it. Every muscle in Amy's body was tense. Her heart was pounding. Her breath was short in her throat.

The trees on each side of them swayed as the unrelenting wind and rain bent them against their will. The road seemed pitch-black beneath the tree canopy. Then there was a brilliant flash of lightning and a clap of thunder so loud it sounded as if a cannon had gone off overhead. Amy screamed and jumped. The horse let out a shriek as a cracking noise echoed through the tunnel.

Straight in front of them, a tree started to fall.

Marion braked violently but the tyres failed to grip the flooded surface. The truck skidded down the road, straight into the path of the tree.

Time slowed down. Powerless to do anything, Amy watched as the tree fell in horrifyingly slow motion towards them. For one wild moment she thought they were just going to get past, but then with a final creaking, crashing noise, the tree collapsed.

With startling clarity, in a single second that seemed to last for ever, Amy saw every little detail, every vein of every green, damp leaf. "*Mom!*" she screamed.

There was a bang, a sickening feeling of falling, and then nothing.

Chapter Four

Amy's eyes fluttered open. White. Everywhere was white. Where was she? She blinked and then focused on a figure sitting at the side of the bed.

"Lou?" she said in surprise.

"Yes, it's me," Lou replied. She looked much the same as ever – corn-coloured hair cut short and forget-me-not-blue eyes – but her face was pale, her eyes strained.

Amy sat up. A sharp pain shot through her head and chest and she caught her breath. "Ow!" she gasped.

Lou put a hand gently on Amy's shoulder. "Careful," she said, "don't try to move too quickly."

"Where am I?" Amy asked, looking round in confusion.

"In the hospital." Lou gently encouraged Amy to lie back against the pillows. "You've been unconscious for eight days. You woke up briefly yesterday." Her eyes searched Amy's.

"Do you remember?"

Amy shook her head. She looked around the room. "Where's Mom?" As soon as the words were out, her eyes widened as the memories returned. The road. The tree. She stared at Lou. "We crashed!"

Lou nodded.

"Is the horse all right?" Amy gasped, ignoring the pain that stabbed in her chest and head as she shot upright again. "And Mom?" She saw Lou look down and her heart suddenly somersaulted with fear. "Lou?" she demanded, her voice catching as she looked at her sister's half-hidden face. "Lou! Where's Mom?"

Lou took a deep breath and slowly met Amy's eyes. "The horse is with Scott Trewin," she said, taking Amy's hand. "He's injured but not too badly, although he's in a bad emotional state." There was a pause. Her voice shook as she squeezed Amy's fingers, "But Mom ... Mom's dead, Amy."

The blood drained from Amy's face. "No," she whispered. She stared at Lou. It couldn't be true. Lou nodded helplessly. Amy's voice rose. "She can't be. Mom can't be dead!"

"She is," Lou said, swallowing hard, her eyes filling with tears. "Her funeral was three days ago."

Amy stared, her breathing getting deeper and deeper.

"You were in a coma," Lou said desperately. "Grandpa and I didn't know when you were going to wake up. We had to go ahead with it." Her eyes searched Amy's. "Oh, Amy, I know how you're feeling..."

"*No!*" Amy's cry erupted out of her with the force of her disbelief and fear. The cry turned into a scream. She couldn't stop it; she didn't want to stop it. She screamed and screamed, only vaguely aware when Lou ran to the door and a nurse came hurrying in. There was a prick in her arm. Her screams faded to a whimper and then sleep closed in on her, dragging her back into the blackness.

For the next few days, Amy lay in her hospital bed and cried as if her heart was going to break. She had broken two ribs and her head ached constantly but she welcomed the physical pain, wanting desperately to block out the anguish she felt inside. It had all been her fault. If she hadn't made Mom go out in the rain then there wouldn't have been an accident and she would still be alive. Over and over again she heard her mother say, "I should never have let you talk me into this." It *was* her fault.

Her grandpa came to visit. "I've brought you some magazines," he said, sitting down beside her. "How are you feeling?"

Amy couldn't answer.

"The horses are fine," he said. "Ty and I have been looking after them. I think they all miss you. And Lou's taken leave from her job to run the business side of things. She's been marvellous. She's so driven – just like your mom." He swallowed. "And you're like your mom, too, honey." He put his hand on hers. "I'm so lucky to have the two of you."

Amy stared down at the white hospital bed.

Jack Bartlett looked at her. His eyes could barely conceal his own grief. "Come on, sweetheart," he said, putting an arm round her and drawing her close. "We'll manage. We *have* to. You, me and Lou, we've still got each other."

Amy shut her eyes. Pain seared through her brain. How *could* they manage? Her mother was dead and *she* had killed her. She pulled away, the words bursting out of her all at once. "It was my fault, Grandpa!"

Jack Bartlett looked confused. "What do you mean?"

"I killed Mom," sobbed Amy. "I made her go out in the rain. She didn't want to go. I made her go."

Her grandpa gripped her shoulder tightly. "Stop that!" he exclaimed intensely. "Amy, you mustn't think like that!"

Amy ignored the pain in her chest as she raised her head off the pillow. "But it's true!" she cried. "I told her we had to go."

Her grandpa pulled her close. Tears were streaming down his face. "Your mother knew the danger but she chose to go because she knew a horse needed her. It was her decision, Amy, not yours." He hugged her fiercely. "And it wasn't your fault."

"It was," Amy said, anguish reducing her voice to a croak. "And I'll never forgive myself."

As the days passed, her eyes ran dry of tears. A terrible numbness stole over her. She couldn't feel, she couldn't think. It was as if everything that was happening to her was happening to someone else. Grandpa and Lou visited each day. Ty came and so did Soraya and Matt. But she found it almost impossible to speak to any of them.

And then, one day, her grandpa and Lou came together. Jack Bartlett stood by the window. Lou perched on the end of the bed and took Amy's hand. "The doctors think that it's time you came home," she said.

"Home?" said Amy bleakly. "I don't have a home any more."

"Of course you do."

Amy looked into Lou's resolute face and slumped back against the bed, hot pain like needles behind her eyes. How could she go back when Mom wasn't going to be there? She turned her head away.

Grandpa stepped forward. "We need you, Amy," he said gently, his voice wavering. "Come home."

Going back to Heartland was worse than Amy could have imagined. As they turned into the driveway, Pegasus and Copper were looking out over their doors. Ty was filling a water bucket at the tap. Everything looked so *normal*. Amy felt her stomach lurch and for a moment she thought she was going to be sick. She flung open the car door and ran into the farmhouse, ignoring the sharp pains in her chest.

She refused to leave it again. She wouldn't go and see the horses. She sat in the kitchen, staring at the floor, wrapped in bleak misery.

"Why don't you come and help me?" Grandpa said the next morning, but Amy stayed put, hunched up in the easy chair.

She watched as Lou tried to make sense of the office that their mother had run. There were papers, notes and cards everywhere, and even the phone numbers for people like the feed merchant and the farrier were all kept in different places. Lou was practical and efficient and appeared to have a system for everything. She did the paperwork and made the phone calls, but the horses she left to Grandpa and Ty. Amy sat in the kitchen, feeling drained and hopeless.

Sometimes she caught Lou glancing in her direction. Sensing the barely hidden exasperation in her eyes, Amy always looked away. She knew Lou thought she should be helping but she couldn't – she couldn't go out to the yard and act as if nothing had happened.

Three days after Amy had come home, Lou turned to her. She had been busy and her eyes were looking strained. "Amy," she said, "can you go and check with Ty which horses need to see the farrier? I can't leave the phone. I'm expecting a call from Bob Shaw, Tarka's owner, any minute now."

Amy shook her head.

"Please, Amy," Lou insisted. "I need to wait for the call."

Amy dug her nails into her palms. "I'm not going out there," she said coolly.

"Oh, for goodness' sake!" Lou said, visibly annoyed.

Pulling on some boots, she hurried out through the door.

A few minutes later, the phone started ringing. Amy stared at it. The shrill bell cried out in the silence of the kitchen but it was as if her legs were frozen. She let it ring and ring.

Suddenly, the door burst open. Lou came dashing in and seized the receiver. "Hello? Heartland," she gasped, her face flushed from running down the yard. There was a second's pause and then she slammed the phone down. "He's gone!" She turned on Amy. "Why didn't you pick it up?" she exclaimed.

Just then, Jack Bartlett came in. Obviously sensing the tension in the air, he cleared his throat. "Ah, Lou. Have you called to confirm the feed delivery?" he asked. "It's just we're getting rather low."

"The feed delivery!" Lou ran a hand through her short hair and stared at him. "What feed delivery?"

"We have a feed delivery every three weeks."

"Well, why didn't someone tell me?" Lou's voice rose angrily. Seeing the surprised expression on their grandpa's face her eyes immediately softened. "Sorry, Grandpa. I didn't mean to snap at you," she said quickly. "I'll sort it out. Don't you worry about a thing."

"You're a good girl, Lou," Jack Bartlett said softly.

Amy felt a sob rising in her throat. Feed deliveries! Phone calls from horse owners! How could they both carry on as if nothing had happened? She got up from her chair and hurried upstairs to her bedroom. Once there, she slumped to the floor, surrounded by a jumble of magazines and clothes, wrapped her arms around her knees and began to sob. What was the matter with them? Mom was dead. Was she the only one who cared?

Amy stayed in her bedroom and didn't go downstairs until the middle of the next morning. When she walked into the kitchen she found Grandpa and Lou sitting at the table. They stopped talking abruptly as she came in.

"Hi, honey," Grandpa said, standing up. "How you doing this morning?"

Amy didn't answer. She just walked over to a chair and sat down.

There was a silence. Amy saw Lou and Grandpa look at each other and then Lou spoke. "Amy," she said quickly. "Grandpa and I have been thinking — it's about time you started to see your friends again."

Amy felt her stomach sink. Soraya and Matt and her other friends from school had been stopping by and phoning up ever since she had got back from the hospital but she had refused to see or speak to any of them, wanting only to be left alone.

"I don't want to," she said.

"Amy!" Lou said. "They're your friends and they want to be around for you." She paused. "Look, we've organized a belated birthday party for you tonight. We thought that way you could see them all together and get over that awkward first meeting."

Amy felt as if she had been punched. "I've told you *already*," she exclaimed in horror, jumping up, "I don't want to see them."

Grandpa came over to her. "Hold on, Amy, Lou's right," he said gently. "You need to start getting on with your life again."

Amy stared at him. *Getting on with my life again!* How could she when Mom was dead?

"We haven't invited loads of people," Lou said. "Just Soraya, Ty, Matt and a few of your other friends that Soraya suggested."

"Well, cancel it!" Amy cried, an awful gnawing feeling growing in the pit of her stomach. "I don't want to see anyone!"

Lou's voice rose in exasperation. "Amy! You can't just opt out of life like this!" Grandpa laid a hand on her arm, and biting her lip, she turned sharply away.

"Grandpa, please…" Amy said.

But much as she argued and pleaded, Lou and Grandpa would not listen. They told her it was for her own good. At last she ran upstairs to her bedroom and refused to come down again for the rest of the day. She was still there at seven o'clock when the guests started arriving.

Grandpa knocked on her bedroom door. "Amy?" He pushed the door open. "Come on," he said gently. "Come downstairs." Amy shook her head miserably. "Please," Grandpa said, holding out his hand. "For me, honey."

Amy looked up at him and suddenly realized how tired he looked. The skin around his eyes was sagging, his brow was furrowed. Very slowly, she took his hand and stood up.

He smiled. "It'll be OK. You'll see."

Amy followed him downstairs, her heart beating fast. As soon as she stepped into the kitchen she knew that it had been a mistake. Her friends stopped talking and stood in silence around the room, awkwardly holding brightly wrapped presents. There was Soraya and Matt, Matt's friend Danny, Ellen and Robyn from her class. Ty stood by the sink next to Lou.

There was a pause. Soraya broke it. She stepped forward, her brown eyes anxiously searching Amy's face. "Hi there," she said, giving her a hug.

As they separated, Amy tried to manage a smile but inside she just wanted to be swallowed up, to escape.

"Hey." Matt came forward. "How you doing?" Amy looked up into his handsome face. His eyes were deep with concern.

"Can I get anyone a drink?" Lou asked. "Amy, what would you like?"

"Nothing," Amy whispered.

There were a couple of seconds of silence. "Drinks, anyone?" Lou said quickly. "Soraya? Ellen? What can I get you?"

As her friends murmured their responses, Amy's eyes strayed to the table.

"Come and sit down, honey," Grandpa said.

Moving as if in a dream, Amy walked over. She looked wordlessly at the pile of presents there.

"Help yourselves to food, everyone," Lou called out. But it seemed as if no one was hungry. The hot dogs and bowls of crisps remained untouched as everyone sat down, looking at Amy with worried eyes.

"Here you are," Matt said, breaking the silence as he handed her his gift, unmistakably a wrapped-up football. He smiled. "Bet you can't guess what it is."

Amy swallowed. "Thanks," she said, trying to force a smile as she took it from him. She stared at the present in her hands. Had it really been only three weeks ago that she and Soraya had laughed about whether Matt would get her a gift or not? It felt like a lifetime away. She looked down, not wanting people to see the tears filling her eyes.

"Here," Ty said suddenly, seeming to sense her distress. He handed her a flat oblong package. "Open mine next." Grateful to have something to concentrate on, Amy fumbled with the paper. She pulled out a framed photograph of Chester. "Oh, Ty, I love it," she whispered, her fingers gripping tightly on to the frame. She glanced up. Ty's eyes met hers, full of understanding.

One by one, Amy unwrapped the other presents. They were just the things she had wanted – riding boots, breeches, riding gloves. Only, now, they didn't seem to matter any more. Eventually Grandpa handed her the last one, which was large and bulky. "This was from your mom," he said. "She bought it the day of the…" his voice trailed off.

Even before her fingers touched it, Amy knew what it was. Trembling slightly, she tore back a strip of the wrapping paper. Blue material showed through. It was the waterproof jacket that she had wanted so badly. It was just too much for Amy to bear. A sob tore through her, and shoving the un-wrapped present away she turned and fled from the room.

A few seconds later, her grandpa appeared in her bed-room doorway. "I'm sorry," he said, coming and sitting beside her on the bed and putting an arm around her shaking shoulders. "I guess we got it wrong. It was too soon for you, wasn't it?"

Through her tears, Amy heard a soft tap on the door. She looked round. It was Soraya.

"Come in," Jack Bartlett said. Getting up, he looked from Soraya to Amy and then walked over to the door. "I'll be downstairs," he said softly, leaving the room.

As soon as he was gone, Soraya ran forward. "Oh, Amy," she said, sitting down and hugging her. "I'm so, so sorry." She leant her head against Amy's so that their hair mingled, black and light brown. "I've been wanting to see you so much, but you just kept saying no," she said. "I'm supposed to be going to camp tomorrow. But I'll stay if you want me to."

"I just want to be left on my own," Amy sobbed.

There was a pause. Realizing how her words must have sounded, Amy looked up. Soraya was looking at her, her eyes brimming with sympathy. "I know," she whispered. "And I guess I'd feel the same."

The next instant they were hugging each other desperately. "I'll write lots," Soraya said through her tears. "If you need me just call, I'll come straight back. I'll always be here for you, Amy."

When Soraya left the room, Amy started to sob again. She was on her own. There was no one who knew how she was feeling, no one who could understand, except Mom, maybe, and she wasn't here any more.

The next afternoon, Lou watched the feed truck arrive. "I hope Ty and Grandpa manage all right," she said, sounding worried. "I'd go and help but the accounts are so behind." She glanced at Amy as if hoping for a response but Amy stayed stubbornly silent. Lou opened her mouth but then seemed to stop herself. She turned sharply away and collecting a big ledger and a pile of papers from one of the drawers in the dresser she sat down at the table. "I cannot believe these aren't computerized," she said.

She quickly leafed through the papers, sorting them into piles. She seemed agitated, slapping the papers down on to the table and glancing every so often at the door as if wondering how the delivery was going. Her mouth looked strained and the areas beneath her blue eyes were shadowed with grey rings of tiredness.

After a few minutes, Lou threw up her hands. "This is impossible! How can I tell who we owe money to? There's no system at all and there're so many invoices missing!"

"They're probably on the bookcase," Amy said flatly. "Or under the easy chair."

"You've got to be kidding!" Lou looked at her incredulously, but got up anyway and started rummaging around under the easy chair. She pulled out a stack of papers. "I don't believe this!" she exclaimed. "Look at them! They're covered in coffee stains."

"So?" said Amy.

"So!" echoed Lou. "So it's dreadful! It's the worst set of accounts that I have ever seen." Her voice rose. "Mom was completely and utterly impractical. How can she have left such an awful mess!"

Amy's emotions overwhelmed her. She jumped to her feet, her eyes blazing with indignant fire. "Because she didn't know she was going to die!" she cried. Anger, pain and misery exploded like a volcano inside her head. "Mom's dead!" she screamed. "Don't you get that? She's dead and all you're worried about is this stupid paperwork! You don't care — do you? You've never cared!"

Lou slammed her fist on the table and stood up. Her face was ashen. "How can you say that?" she gasped, her voice shaking. "Have you *any* idea how hard it is for me to try and carry on? You're so selfish, Amy!" Amy tried to interrupt but Lou wouldn't let her. "Yes, you are!" she cried. "You don't think about Grandpa or Ty or anyone else. The only person you think about is poor Amy Fleming. And all you want to do is mope around feeling sorry for yourself. Well, moping around isn't going to bring Mom back, and I can tell you one thing: if Mom was here now and you were dead she'd be out there looking after those horses! You say *I* don't care. Well, take a look at *yourself*, Amy! Just take a look at yourself!"

For a moment they stared at each other. Amy felt all the colour drain out of her face. Lou suddenly looked appalled. "Amy..." she said, quickly stepping forward. "Amy, I'm so..."

"Leave me alone!" Amy hissed, jumping away.

"Try to understand..." Lou begged.

"*You* try to understand!" Amy howled. "Just leave me alone!" Turning, she raced out of the kitchen and up the stairs to her bedroom. Slamming the door, she flung herself on to her bed and gave way to her grief.

Lou came up and knocked softly on the door. A little while later Grandpa did the same but Amy refused to let either of them in. "Oh, Mom," she sobbed wildly, "Mom! Why aren't you here?"

It was just getting light outside when Amy woke up. Her eyes were sore, her face felt rough with tears. She stood up and looked out of the window. All was silent. She felt empty inside. Her life seemed to stretch out bleakly ahead. No one understood her any more. There was no one who could take her mom's place.

Then she noticed Pegasus looking over his door. Amy's heart gave a leap as she saw the big grey head, the half-pricked ears – watching, waiting. And suddenly it hit her like a thump in the stomach. Of course – why hadn't she thought about him before?

She crept downstairs, silently opened the back door and hurried across the yard. Pegasus pricked his ears and snorted with delight at the sight of her. She eased back the bolt on his door and let herself in. The warmth of his familiar stall enveloped her. Pegasus bent his head enquiringly, breathing out love and trust.

She flung her arms around his neck. "Oh, Pegasus!" she said desperately. "What am I going to do?"

Pegasus' neck was warm and solid. His mane scratched against her face. "We've lost her," Amy whispered, her voice breaking. "Things will never be the same again. It's just you and me now."

Pegasus snorted softly.

"Just you and me." As Amy painfully repeated the words, she thought about everything she and her mom had done together, about everything they had meant to each other. And as she drew comfort from Pegasus' presence, she thought about Lou's words. Was she right? *Was* she being selfish?

Her hands start to work absent-mindedly on Pegasus' neck. Small circles, light pressure, just like Mom had shown her. Pegasus liked that. Amy smiled as she felt him relax beneath her touch, and as her hands moved she felt her own tension start to ease.

The time passed. The sun rose. She heard her grandpa's old-fashioned alarm clock ring in the house. Amy kissed Pegasus on the nose and slipped out of his loose box. Unnoticed she hurried back to her room.

She lay on her bed, feeling much calmer. It had started to rain. She heard Grandpa and Lou get up. Heard the clank of feed buckets and the stamping of hooves. Moving to the window and standing at the side of the curtains, she watched as her grandpa began to feed the horses and Ty arrived. It was a dull day, the clouds were grey and a fine drizzle was falling. Downstairs Lou was getting breakfast ready. A normal day had begun.

A few minutes later, she saw Lou come outside and go over to chat with Grandpa. Turning slowly, Amy walked out of her room and down the winding staircase. As she reached the hall she stopped. Someone had put her birthday present from Mom on the hall table. It was still wrapped with the gift card on top. Amy swallowed and then slowly moved towards it. She paused before reaching out with trembling fingers to lift the card.

Just at that moment the telephone in the kitchen rang out shrilly. Amy jumped and turned. Should she answer it? She was about to go through to the kitchen when she heard the back door opening and checked herself.

"Hello, Heartland," she heard Ty say cheerfully. There was a silence. When he spoke again the tone of his voice had changed dramatically. "Yes … I know the place," he said, sounding quick and serious. "OK. We'll be there as soon as possible." There was the click of the receiver and then the sound of the back door being thrown open. "Jack!" he shouted. "You'd better come here!"

Amy hesitated in the hall. *What was happening?* There were running footsteps and the sound of Lou and Grandpa entering the house. "What's the matter, Ty?" she heard her grandpa demand.

"That was the police!" Ty exclaimed. "They've just been up to old Mrs Bell's house. They broke in and found her inside." He paused. "She's been dead for several weeks."

Dead! Amy's hand flew to her mouth.

"Oh no!" she heard Lou gasp. "That's awful!"

"Eric alerted them when he went up there this morning on his post-round," Ty continued quickly. "He's been away on holiday for two weeks and no one else has been near the place."

"Of course, ordinarily Amy would have gone over there," Grandpa groaned. "Oh my – how awful."

"It gets worse." Ty said grimly. "It's not just Mrs Bell. The police were ringing about Sugarfoot."

Amy's heart somersaulted. *Sugarfoot!*

"The little Shetland?" Grandpa said.

"Yes. He's been shut in his stable," Ty said. "No food and very little water. The police say he's in really bad shape, half starved and very frightened. They've called Scott Trewin, but wanted to know if one of us could meet him up there."

Amy felt a trembling sob rise through her. Oh, poor little Sugarfoot! Her heart ached for the tiny pony — alone, starved, frightened...

"Will you go?" she heard Grandpa saying to Ty.

"Sure," Ty said. "Sugarfoot doesn't know me, but I guess that can't be helped."

"I'll take you up there," said Lou.

Amy imagined how Sugarfoot would feel when Ty, whom he didn't know or trust, tried to put him in a trailer and take him away from the only home he had ever known. Her heart began to beat fast. She looked round the hall desperately and as she did so her eyes fell on the present again. *Mom*, she thought, *Mom, what would you do?* Almost without thinking she lifted the card and read:

> *To my dear Amy,*
> *Keep trusting those instincts and together we'll achieve*
> *our dreams.*
> *Happy Birthday!*
> *Love and hugs, Mom.*

The words seemed to hit Amy with the force of a sledge-hammer. *Together*. Tears sprang to her eyes as she thought about the dreams she and Mom had shared, the plans they had made.

"I guess I'd better get going," she heard Ty say in the kitchen.

Suddenly Amy knew what she had to do. Swiftly, she tore the wrapping paper off the coat and slipped it on. The card lay on the table. Touching it, Amy swallowed her tears. "I'm doing this for you, Mom," she whispered. "For our dreams."

Grandpa, Lou and Ty all jumped slightly as Amy appeared in the kitchen doorway. She put up a hand to stop them saying anything.

"I'll go," she said.

Chapter Five

Lou and Amy walked round the house to where the pick-up and trailer were parked. Neither of them spoke. Their angry words from the day before seemed to hang in the air between them like an invisible barrier. Ignoring Amy, Lou picked her way cautiously through the long, damp grass in her open-toed shoes and unlocked the door. Amy suddenly stopped. The side of the truck was freshly repaired and painted.

Lou looked round. "What are we…" Her words trailed off as she followed the direction of Amy's gaze. "Oh," she said, her face instantly softening. "I'm sorry. I didn't think." She closed the door to the truck and pocketed the keys. "Look, you don't have to come," she said. "I'm sure Ty could manage."

Amy swallowed and shook her head. She dug her hands

deeper into the pockets of her coat. "No," she said. "I have to help Sugarfoot."

She walked slowly up to the truck and got in, her heart pounding in her chest. Still looking at her anxiously, Lou started the engine. Every bump and jolt as they drove down the driveway flashed another scene of the accident in Amy's mind. The windscreen wipers swept across the glass and she gripped the seat tightly, forcing herself to think about Sugarfoot.

As they made the turn out of the driveway Lou spoke awkwardly to Amy. "I'm really sorry about yesterday," she said. "I shouldn't have said those things."

Amy looked at her hands in her lap. "It's OK."

There was a weighted silence. The words that had passed between them couldn't be unsaid. She *could* try to reassure Lou now, but although the gap that separated them was only the width of a seat, emotionally it felt as vast as an ocean. They drove the rest of the way in silence, apart from the few whispered directions that Amy gave.

"Where's the stable?" Lou asked, as she parked the trailer outside Mrs Bell's house.

Amy pulled the door open. "At the back!" she said, jumping out into the drizzle and setting off round the house. As she ran up the path to the barn, a strong smell of manure and urine hit her. She hesitated for a moment a short distance from the half-door. What would she see when she looked inside? Biting her lip, she stepped forward.

"Oh, Sugarfoot!" a horrified whisper escaped her. The little Shetland stood in the centre of the floor, his head drooping to the ground. His ribs stuck out, his flanks were hollowed and his coat was matted with clumps of mud. The stench in the stable was almost unbearable.

With trembling fingers, Amy unbolted the door and pulled it open. The pony's chestnut ears flickered and with the greatest of efforts he raised his head. His dull eyes fixed on Amy and with a glimmer of recognition he whickered hoarsely. Ignoring the muck, she crouched beside him, her hands reaching up to gently touch his head and neck. He moved his ears slightly as if to acknowledge her. She could hardly believe the change in him.

"Amy?" It was Lou, calling from the garden.

She stood up and went to the stable door. "Over here!"

Lou walked gingerly up the overgrown path. "Should I turn the trailer round before you put him in or should I...." Her voice stopped abruptly as she focused on Sugarfoot. She stared at the emaciated little horse and drew in her breath sharply. "Oh, no!" Lou stepped closer and for a moment the two of them said nothing. "This is dreadful!" Lou eventually gasped, tears filling her eyes.

Just then there was a shout from the bottom of the garden. "Amy – are you there?" Amy and Lou turned.

"Scott!" Amy said, seeing the tall figure of Scott Trewin striding up the garden towards them. He stopped in front of her and looked down at her with concern in his eyes. "How are you doing?"

"I'm fine," Amy brushed off the question. She wanted to put her own problems on hold and deal with the immediate situation. "It's Sugarfoot we have to worry about." She moved to let him look in the stable, and then realized that Lou was still standing there and hastily introduced them, "Oh, this is Lou. My sister."

Scott and Lou acknowledged each other. "We've met," Scott said.

Amy suddenly realized that Scott was still looking after the stallion that she and her mother had picked up in the trailer that night on Clairdale Ridge. And of course, Lou and Scott would have met before – he would have gone to their mother's funeral. She pushed the thought away. It wasn't something she wanted to think about right now.

Scott went into the stable and glanced around. "OK, let's try and get him out of here. Amy, get ready to support Sugarfoot on that side and gently encourage him to move. Remember he'll be very weak."

Amy and Scott stood either side of the little pony's head and encouraged him forward. Painfully, step by step, he slowly left his stable. Lou watched for a moment or two and then disappeared down the garden path. Amy hardly noticed her go, she was too busy concentrating all her attention on Sugarfoot.

"OK," Scott said as they got him out on to the grass. "Let's check him over." He gently ran his hands over the pony's body and then took his pulse and heart-rate.

Amy caressed Sugarfoot's tiny ears to soothe him. All the time Scott was examining him the pony stood still, staring straight ahead. Amy was amazed that he didn't seem interested in the lush grass all around him.

Scott looked inside the stable again. "Well, he's had water," he said, pointing to a drainpipe that ran from the side of the roof and emptied into a pail in the stable. "If it hadn't been for that…" He shook his head. Amy knew what he meant. No horse could survive without water for more than a couple of days in the heat of the summer. "I think the best thing we can do is to get him back to Heartland and see what you guys can do for him. There are no signs of secondary problems at the moment. As long as we can get him eating his chances are good."

"I'll get him eating," Amy said confidently. She stroked Sugarfoot's head. She was going to make him better.

"OK, then," Scott said with a smile. "Let's get him down to the trailer."

Lou was waiting for them. She had lowered the ramp, and now she watched as Amy and Scott tried to coax the little Shetland into the back.

Sugarfoot took a few tentative steps and then hesitated, going in only when Amy pulled on his halter and Scott encouraged him from behind.

"Can you do anything for him?" Lou asked Scott

anxiously, as the pony stepped the last of the way inside.

"Well, other than being under-nourished there seems to be nothing wrong with him," Scott answered, coming down the ramp. His voice sounded cold. "Leave it to Amy. She knows what to do." Amy frowned as she lifted the ramp. It wasn't like Scott to be so reserved. He turned to her as she started fastening the bolts. "Give me a ring if you're worried about anything, OK?" he said, sounding more like his normal self. "Otherwise I'll stop by in the morning."

Amy nodded. "OK. See you tomorrow, then."

"Yeah, tomorrow." Scott nodded briefly at Lou and then strode off to his car.

When they arrived back at Heartland, Amy was relieved to find that Ty had put down a thick bed of straw in one of the stalls in the back barn. With his usual patience he helped Amy get Sugarfoot down the ramp and into the stall. The little Shetland walked in and then lay down immediately, his nose resting on the straw and his eyes half closed.

"Looks like he could use some feeding up," Ty said, running his eyes over Sugarfoot's sticking-out ribs. The concern on his face belied his casual words.

Amy nodded. "I'll go and make him a bran mash to start him off. Is there any beet pulp soaked?"

Ty nodded. "In the feed-room. I'll go and fetch some hay."

Amy smiled at him gratefully. "Thanks, Ty." She was relieved that he hadn't made a song and dance about her being out of the house and in the yard again. He simply seemed to accept it, immediately concentrating on the task of getting Sugarfoot better.

She went to the feed-room and filled a bucket with bran and put the kettle on the stove. As she waited for it to boil, she chopped up some carrots and mixed them with a scoop of beet pulp and a handful of barley into the bran. She knew it was essential not to over-feed a horse in Sugarfoot's condition. Having not eaten for so long, his stomach wouldn't be able to cope with a large amount of food. The progress had to be slow and steady, the quantity gradually increased.

She went to the cabinet in the corner of the room. It contained books on herbal remedies, dried herbs, flower essences, ointments and aromatherapy oils. It was so familiar to Amy. Marion had carefully taught her all she knew about natural remedies.

Ignoring a lump rising in her throat, Amy consulted her mom's notebook and then added fenugreek seeds to the feed to make it more appetizing for the little pony, some garlic powder to help his digestion and a handful of chopped rosehip shells, rich in vitamins.

At last the feed was ready and Amy carried it round to Sugarfoot's stable, placing it on the floor by his nose. He lifted his head slightly when she came in. "Here you go, boy," she said, crouching down beside him to stroke his neck. He sniffed at the bucket and then looked away.

"Come on, Sugarfoot," she said, feeling surprised that he

needed any encouragement. It was rare that a horse refused a bran mash. She picked out a handful of food and held it out to the little pony. His lips snuffled at her hand as he ate a piece of carrot. She reached for another handful. Sugarfoot nibbled a bit more but after the third handful he turned his head away again.

Amy sat back, feeling perplexed. Maybe it was just too soon after his journey, maybe he needed more time to settle in. Leaving the pail beside him she fetched a grooming bucket. Sitting next to him on the straw, she very gently started to comb through his coat and unknot the tangles in his mane and tail.

By the evening, Sugarfoot's appearance was better but he still had not eaten more than a few handfuls of food. Amy was beginning to feel concerned.

"Still no luck?" Ty asked, popping his head over the stall door before he left for the day. Amy shook her head.

"Guess he just needs an untroubled night's sleep," Ty said.

"Guess so." Amy stood up and looked at the little pony. He was resting his head on the straw, his eyes half closed. But what if he *didn't* start eating tomorrow — what would she do then?

Chapter Six

Amy woke up earlier than usual the next morning. As soon as she opened her eyes she thought about Sugarfoot. How would he be today? Pushing back the covers, she jumped up, hurriedly got dressed and ran down the stairs and out into the yard. The horses pricked up their ears and whinnied in greeting as she passed.

But Sugarfoot was still lying in his stall, his legs curled up underneath him, looking tinier than ever. Amy unbolted the stall door. Her heart sank when she saw that his feed and hay had remained untouched. His appetite obviously hadn't returned yet.

She knelt down beside him. His eyes flickered on her for a moment and then dropped dully. Amy gently stroked his mane and smoothed his thick cream-coloured forelock away from his eyes. With a sigh, Sugarfoot leant his muzzle on her knee. Her fingers started to gently massage his ears, tiny feather-light circles, up to the base and down to the tip. Focusing entirely on her work, Amy didn't hear the footsteps coming towards the stall.

"Hi."

Amy jumped. Lou stood on the other side of the stall door looking in.

Amy's grey eyes widened in astonishment. "Lou!" Lou *never* came into the barn.

Lou sighed. "I couldn't sleep," she said. "And then I saw you coming over here from the house." She looked at Sugarfoot. "How is he?"

"He still hasn't eaten," Amy said, trying not to sound surprised.

Lou frowned. "But why not? He must be starving."

Amy knew Lou's reaction was logical and she tried to explain as best she could. "Sometimes, if they're in shock, horses don't eat. Sugarfoot's traumatized. He doesn't know why he was locked in his stable for so long or why he's been brought here. He's only ever really known life with Mrs Bell. She treated him just like a pet, she used to talk to him and let him in the house. Now Mrs Bell's gone and I guess that's the only thing he's really aware of."

"And the poor thing has no home to go to any more," Lou said softly. She looked at Sugarfoot for a moment and then her gaze flickered to Amy, a certain respect showing in her eyes. "You know a lot about this, don't you, Amy?"

"Mom taught me," Amy said. She swallowed and struggled with the emotion that suddenly threatened to engulf her. For a long moment she was lost in her own thoughts.

"He will get better, won't he?" Lou said eventually, breaking the silence.

Amy looked at the little Shetland. She desperately wanted to believe he would but at the same time she couldn't deny the feeling of foreboding that seemed lodged in the deepest corner of her heart.

Lou saw her hesitation and it was enough. "Why do horses always cause so much heartache?" she said bitterly, stepping back from the door.

"They don't *always*," Amy said, looking at her quickly. "Most of the time they give so much to the people they love."

"OK, but they take away a lot more," Lou replied coldly, and walked away.

Lou would never understand, Amy thought. Shaking her head, she resumed massaging Sugarfoot's ears.

At six o'clock, Amy left the little pony and set to work getting the breakfast feeds ready. She added a handful of dried mint to the top of Sugarfoot's bran mash, hoping that it might tempt him to eat, but when she put the pail in his stall he turned his head away. Amy sighed and finished off feeding the other horses. She would just have to try something else.

After filling the water buckets and giving Sundance – who was whinnying frantically every time he saw her – some attention, she went into the house for breakfast. Lou was talking on the phone. Grandpa was sitting at the table finishing a mug of coffee. Amy kicked off her trainers at the door and started to talk about Sugarfoot as she padded across the floor in her socks.

Lou put her hand over the mouthpiece. "Can you be quiet?" she hissed. "I'm trying to have a conversation!"

"It's Carl," Grandpa winked at Amy.

"Oh," she said, unimpressed. She poured herself a glass of orange juice and sat down.

"Yes, I know," Lou was saying. "I miss you too."

Amy pulled a face at her grandpa. He frowned at her but she could see the twinkle in his eyes. She guessed that he hadn't taken to Carl any more than she had.

"I know. It's difficult," Lou said. There was a pause. "Yes, soon. I promise." Looking over her shoulder she met Amy's gaze and turned her back. "Look, I can't talk now. But I promise it won't be long." She paused and said softly, "Yeah, me too. Bye." She put the phone down and her gaze fell on Amy's trainers in front of her on the floor. "Amy, do you have to leave everything lying round for other people to pick up?"

"I'm going out again in a minute," Amy protested.

"And how was Carl?" Grandpa queried, as Lou moved the offending trainers.

"Fine, thanks." She smiled. "Keen to know when I'm going back."

"Going back?" Amy echoed, the glass of orange juice stopping halfway to her mouth.

"Yes." Lou frowned. "You didn't think I was going to stay, did you? My life's in Manhattan. I've got my job and Carl and my apartment."

Amy didn't know what to say. She hadn't really given it much thought. She had just assumed that Lou *would* be staying with them.

Obviously seeing the expression on her face, Lou eyes softened. "Don't worry. I'm not just going to desert you," she said. "I'll still do all the paperwork – I can do it in the evenings. And I'm working out a business plan for here." She folded her arms. "You and Grandpa will have to be a lot more practical in future."

"Practical?" Amy echoed, shooting a look at Grandpa. She had a horrible feeling that she wasn't going to like Lou's plan.

"Yes, practical," Lou said firmly, collecting the breakfast dishes from the table and carrying them over to the sink. "Things are going to have to change round here." She paused by the window. "There's someone coming up the driveway. I think it's your friend Matt."

Immediately pushing Lou's "practical" plans to the back of her mind, Amy hurried to the window in surprise. Lou was right, it *was* Matt! Forgetting breakfast, Amy went out of the back door.

Seeing her, Matt waved. "Hey, stranger!" he said.

"Matt!" Amy exclaimed. She hadn't seen any of her friends since her disastrous birthday party. "What are you doing here?"

Matt jogged over. "I came to see you. I thought you could do with the company." His voice softened and he looked at her with concern in his eyes. "How've you been?"

"OK," Amy said quickly. For a moment she thought Matt was going to hug her. She hurriedly started to tell him about Sugarfoot.

"I heard. Scott told me," Matt said. "Can I see him?"

"Sure. He's in the back barn." Amy said.

Matt followed her up to the Shetland's stall. He whistled softly under his breath when he saw the pony's emaciated state. "He's bad."

"I've been trying to get him to eat, but he just won't," Amy explained. "I think it's time to have another look through Mom's books."

Taking a pile of books down from the shelf in the tackroom, Amy said, "I want to try wormwood. It's supposed to encourage appetite and we've got some in the herb patch."

"Well, if you want to go and pick some I'll read through these and see what else might work," Matt said, opening the first book.

"Are you sure?" Amy asked.

"Sure," Matt said, flicking through the pages. "I like books like this. Alternative therapies are great." He grinned up at her. "Anyhow, I'd like to help."

By the time Amy came back, Matt already had a page of scribbled notes. "There's quite a few different things for increasing appetite," he told her. "But a wormwood infusion seems to be the most popular."

"Let's hope it works then," Amy said, filling up the kettle. She tore up a handful of the leaves and then put them in a bowl with the water when it had boiled. They left the infusion to stand for fifteen minutes and then carried it up to the barn.

Sugarfoot didn't even raise his head as they came in. Amy knelt down beside him on the straw but no amount of coaxing could persuade him to drink.

"If only he'd take even a tiny bit," Amy said. "Come on, Sugarfoot." But the little pony just lay there. He seemed totally uninterested.

"We could get a syringe and squirt it into his mouth," Matt suggested

Amy shook her head. "If he *won't* eat it then he's telling us that it's not what he needs."

Matt frowned at her. "But surely if it's going to help him then you should try and get some of it down him."

Amy shook her head. "You have to trust the horse – listen to him." The words caught in her throat. She could almost imagine Mom standing there, saying the same thing. *Listen to the horses*, her soft voice spoke in Amy's thoughts, *they know what they need*. Looking at Matt's puzzled face, she could see that he didn't understand.

"Come on," she said, forcing herself to get to her feet, "let's go and find something else to try."

But no matter how many other herbal remedies they tried, Sugarfoot simply turned his head away. Amy had never known a horse refuse absolutely everything in this way. Her frustration mounted. There had to be *something* they could do.

Just before lunchtime, Scott arrived. One look at the full feed bucket told him the news. "So he hasn't eaten anything yet?" he said to Amy and Matt.

Amy shook her head and described the herbs she had been trying. "He won't eat any of them," she said. "What can we do, Scott?"

Scott gently rubbed Sugarfoot's neck. "Just keep on trying, I guess." His eyes looked grave. "But if he's going to recover then he has to start eating. His immune system will have weakened. Soon, we'll be dealing with secondary problems – pneumonia, other respiratory infections." He stood up and brushed the straw off his clothes. "Come on, let's leave him to rest."

"Do you want a drink?" Amy asked as they walked down the yard.

Scott nodded. "Thanks."

They headed into the house. Amy dropped her sweatshirt by the door. "Coke, OK?" she said, going over to the fridge.

"Fine," said Matt.

Scott nodded. "Sure." He looked at the table covered with forms and files arranged in neat piles. "Somebody's busy."

Amy handed Scott and Matt a can each and opened one for herself. "Sit down," she offered, pushing the papers to one side with her arm just as Lou came into the kitchen.

"Mind those papers!" she cried. "They're for work." Amy had placed her drink on a pile and a damp ring had already spread out at the bottom of the can. "Amy!" Lou exclaimed, snatching up the can. "These are important!" She saw Amy's sweatshirt. "And do you have to leave your clothes in the middle of the floor!"

"Sorry," Amy said.

Lou sighed. "I hope you'll be a bit tidier when Carl comes to stay."

"Carl!" Amy echoed. "He's coming here?"

"Yes. We discussed it this morning. He's coming in two weeks."

"Oh, great," Amy muttered.

Lou ignored her and turned to Scott who was still standing by the fridge. "Hello," she said brightly. "How are you, Scott?"

"Fine, thank you," he said, his voice reserved.

"Maybe you can help me. I'm trying to think of a decent restaurant that Carl and I can go to. I mean, if I were in Manhattan I wouldn't have a problem." She laughed. "There you can't escape from the things. But here! Well, I don't know how you manage!" She looked at Scott. "Is there anywhere you would suggest?"

"Not really," Scott's voice was cool. "I don't have much

time to eat out." Amy looked at him in surprise. Scott was normally so warm and friendly, but now he was looking distinctly steely-eyed.

"Oh, right," Lou said, looking rather taken aback. "Fine. I'll just look in a guide book or ask Grandpa."

Scott turned to Amy. "Well, I'd better get going. I'll stop by again tomorrow." He looked at Matt. "Are you coming with me or staying here?"

"I'll come," Matt said. "I've promised to help Dad in the garden this afternoon." He looked at Amy. "But I'll come round again soon. OK?"

"OK," she smiled.

Scott nodded briskly to Lou and strode out to the car with Matt following. Amy frowned as she stood in the doorway and watched them get into the car. What was up with Scott? He had been so cool towards Lou that he had been almost rude. It wasn't like him at all. She shrugged and went back inside. Maybe he just found it difficult to relate to people who didn't love and understand horses the way he did.

Amy made herself a sandwich and set off up the yard, eating it as she walked. There was so much to do — stalls to be mucked out and grooming to be done, and that was just the start of it. There were also horses to be exercised as well as the ones who needed working in the ring, and Sundance — who was so delighted to have her back on the yard that he galloped to the fence every time he saw her. She stopped to feed Pegasus the crusts from her sandwich and for the first time began to wonder how she, Grandpa and Ty would cope with all the work involved with looking after a yardful of horses. Thank goodness she had the long summer holiday to concentrate on Heartland.

The livery horses – those who had come to be cured of behavioural problems – had all returned to their homes after the accident. But that still left eight horses and seven ponies needing attention, many of whom required substantial work if they were going to be successfully re-homed.

Amy patted Pegasus. How would they manage? She came to a decision. The only thing to do was to keep more of the horses out at grass full-time rather than stabling them. That way, less time would be needed on the stalls and she and Ty could spend more time working on the horses who needed it. But what would happen when she went back to school in the autumn? And what about in the winter when it would be too cold to keep the horses out all of the time? They needed someone else to help, but they would never be able to afford another paid stable-hand. If only Lou would stay.

"We'll manage," Amy thought aloud. After all, they always had done in the past. Things had been tough before but they had come right in the end.

She gave Pegasus one last pat and went to find Ty.

He was filling hay nets in the barn. Amy told him about her plan to keep more of the horses out in the paddocks.

"Mm, it's a good idea," he said, stopping and folding his arms. "We definitely need to do something to cut our workload down. Which ones do you reckon?"

"I thought Jake, Moochie…" She was interrupted by the sound of the phone ringing. "I'll get it!" she said. She raced down the yard and into the kitchen. Lou and Grandpa had gone out together to do the grocery shopping.

"Heartland," she gasped.

"Hi." It was a man's voice on the other end. "My name's Nick Halliwell. I'm ringing up about a horse of mine. I was hoping you could help…"

Ten minutes later, Amy returned to the barn. Ty had finished the hay nets and was sweeping up the loose hay from the ground.

"Anyone interesting?" he said, leaning on the brush.

"Um … yes." She looked down at her hands. "It was a man about a horse."

"A rescue?"

"No, a horse that won't go in a trailer."

"Oh," Ty started sweeping again. "Did you suggest anyone else? There's Ridgeway Farm. They're a little far, but they're supposed to be reasonable." When she didn't say anything, he looked at her. "Amy, you didn't…"

She nodded rather sheepishly. "I said he could come here."

Chapter Seven

It didn't take Amy long to persuade Ty to come round to the idea. "It's not going to be that much work. It's only getting the horse to go in a trailer. The owner sounded really desperate – I couldn't turn him down. And anyway, it will bring some money in."

Ty sighed with resignation. "Well, I guess you're right," he said, picking up the brush again to finish off the sweeping. "So how old is this horse?"

"Five. He's a show-jumper. His owner had seen the article in *Horse Life*. I told him about Mom, but he still wanted us to have a try," her voice wavered. She looked at Ty.

"So when's it coming?" Ty asked quickly.

"Tomorrow."

"Tomorrow!"

"I'll go and get a stall ready now," she said.

As Amy shook out the fresh straw, she wondered for a moment if she had done the right thing. Yes, she was sure she had – Heartland needed as many paying horses as they could get and the man had sounded so grateful when she had said yes. "He's a very special horse," he had told her. Amy smiled to herself. *Everyone* always thought their own horse was the most special horse in the world. Still, she had liked the sound of his voice. She would go with her gut reaction on this one. And saying yes to Nick Halliwell had definitely felt like the right thing to do.

She waited until supper time to break the news to Lou and Grandpa. "A new horse is coming tomorrow," she said when they were all sitting round the table.

"A new horse?" Grandpa echoed.

"Yes. Its owner rang today; he said that it wouldn't go in a trailer and asked if we could help." Amy paused. "I said yes." She looked at them both. Grandpa was shaking his head in amused exasperation but Lou was staring at her as though she had grown two heads.

"You told someone that we could take on another horse?" she exclaimed, as if Amy had just said that she could fly.

Amy nodded. "I thought we could use the money, and it's an easy problem to cure."

"But Amy, what about the time and work involved?" Lou lifted her hands incredulously, her voice rising. "There are already fifteen horses out there that aren't getting the attention they need. Ty's worked off his feet as it is and Grandpa has no time to himself these days!"

"We'll manage," Amy said, feeling optimistic. "After all, we're going to have to start taking in horses again at some point."

"No, we aren't!" Lou cried. Amy stared at her. Her face was burning with emotion. "Amy! Heartland can't carry on as it was before. I'm amazed that you can't see that! Things have to change…"

"Lou," Jack Bartlett interrupted warningly.

Lou swung round. "We should tell her, Grandpa."

"What?" Amy asked, looking enquiringly from one to the other. As she saw a look pass between them, her heart started to speed up. "Tell me what?" Her voice rose. "What are you talking about?"

Lou glanced at their grandpa. He nodded slightly as if giving her permission to go ahead. "I told you this morning that I'd been making some plans," she said to Amy. "I've been discussing them this afternoon with Grandpa. Without Mom, Heartland can't continue to be run the way it was."

"Why not?" Amy demanded.

"Time, Amy. Time, money and manpower. You, Grandpa and Ty can't possibly manage all the horses between you."

"We can!" Even as she said the words Amy knew that Lou was right, but she was determined to try and fight her corner. She couldn't bear for things to change even more than they had already. "Well, *you* could stay for a start!"

Lou frowned. "I've told you, my life's in New York. Not here. And anyway, Amy, it's the money as well. Most of the money coming in was from the problem horses that Mom dealt with. Without her, that line of income is closed. People aren't going to bring their horses here any more."

"They are!" Amy cried. "What about this one that's coming tomorrow?"

"It's a one-off. Let's face it, people brought their horses here because of Mom."

"So what are you saying?" Amy stared at her incredulously. "We close Heartland?"

"Well, not close it, exactly." Lou appeared to be choosing her words carefully. "No. Think of it more as *down-sizing*. We re-home each of the horses as they become ready and don't take any new ones in. By the autumn, we're left with the six or so permanent residents that can't be re-homed. You get to keep Heartland but on a much smaller scale."

Amy jumped to her feet. "No!"

"Amy, be sensible," Lou said. "You have to admit it, it's the practical solution."

"Grandpa, do you agree with this?" Amy turned to her grandpa for support.

"Lou has a point, Amy," he said, sighing. "Come the fall, you'll be in school all day. Ty can't cope with fifteen horses on his own. If we rent out the extra land, that should bring in enough money to pay for the upkeep of the remaining horses."

Amy stared at him. She felt as though a knife had just been twisted into her heart. "How could you?" she whispered, her voice full of hurt and bewilderment. She jumped to her feet, her voice rising. "How *could* you do this to me? And how could you do it to Mom?"

"Amy..." he began.

"I thought you loved this place as much as I do!" she yelled.

Lou jumped to her feet angrily. "Don't you dare speak to Grandpa like that!"

Amy swung round. "I hate you!" she screamed. "Why don't you just go back to your fancy job in New York and stay there! Your *business* here is finished!"

With an agonized sob Amy ran out of the kitchen, slamming the door. She ran blindly, tears streaming down her face as she headed for Pegasus' stall. She flung her arms round the horse's neck.

A few minutes later, quiet footsteps stopped outside the stall door. "Amy?" It was Grandpa.

"Go away," she sobbed.

But Jack Bartlett let himself into the stall and laid a hand on her shoulder. She flinched at his touch but then seeing his face, so concerned and hurt, she couldn't help but throw herself into his arms. "Oh, Grandpa, I can't bear it. I really can't!"

Grandpa held Amy close, letting her cry, gently stroking her hair. Beside them, Pegasus whickered softly into the warmth of the night.

*　*　*

Amy came downstairs the following morning, her eyes red and her face pale. She found Lou in the kitchen, sitting at the table, listlessly stirring a spoon round and round in her mug of coffee. Their eyes met.

"Amy," Lou said, standing up.

Ignoring her, Amy walked through the kitchen and out of the back door, slamming it behind her.

She went straight to Sugarfoot's stall. As soon as she saw the little pony lying so quietly in the straw, his bucket of food untouched, she pushed her own troubles to the back of her mind. He looked so weak. She hurried to fetch some more wormwood from the garden and offered him a few of the fresh leaves. His lips grazed over her palm, scattering the leaves on to the ground. "You're supposed to *eat* them, Sugarfoot," Amy said, feeling desperation start to grow in her as she collected them up. "If you tried them they might help you get your appetite back." Sugarfoot looked at her with dull brown eyes.

She paused for a moment, the truth suddenly becoming clear. Sugarfoot didn't want to get his appetite back. He didn't want to get better. He was missing Mrs Bell so much that he wanted to die himself. If Amy was ever going to get him to eat, she would have to find a way to ease his grief.

Ignoring the other horses that kicked on their doors and whinnied hopefully as she went past, she hurried to the feed-room and went to the corner cabinet. She opened one of her

92

mom's books and found the chapter on emotional problems. It recommended the use of flower remedies and aroma-therapy oils. Deciding to start with rescue remedy, which was supposed to help with emotional shock, Amy found the dark-brown bottle in the cabinet and hurried back to Sugarfoot's stall. She placed two drops from the bottle on the back of her hand and offered it to him. He sniffed and then listlessly licked them off.

Amy let out a sigh of relief. It was a start, at least. Adding ten drops to his water bucket she left his stall. Now all she could do was wait and see what happened.

Ty arrived soon after and the pair of them set to work, mucking out the stalls. As Amy worked she couldn't stop thinking about Sugarfoot – would the rescue remedy help? Her thoughts were interrupted by the sound of hooves coming up the drive. A chestnut horse clattered into the yard, ridden by a young man.

"Hey!" Amy said curiously, going to meet the rider.

"Are you Amy?" he asked. She nodded. The man dismounted and held out his hand. "Taylor Ellis. This is Star. Mr Halliwell sent me over with him."

Star! The horse that had come to have its problem with trailers cured. "Oh, right," Amy said, looking at the horse's warm neck. "How long did it take you to get here?"

"A couple of hours." Taylor obviously registered her surprised expression. "But it would have taken twice that to get him into a trailer. He goes crazy. Just lies down and refuses to move. We're really hoping that you have some luck with him."

Amy looked at the thoroughbred horse. His head was finely chiselled, his eyes large and calm. She dug in her pocket and produced a mint that he gracefully accepted. "Oh, we will," she said, gently touching Star's face and noticing how he pushed against her in a friendly way.

Taylor raised his eyebrows slightly and looked as if he was going to say something, but just then a car came up the drive. "Here's my lift," he said. "Nick said he'd call you tonight." He gave Star a quick pat. "He's got great plans for this horse."

Amy helped unload Star's tack and rugs from the car and then put the horse in the stall next to Pegasus. She would leave him to settle in and later that day they would start working together.

After lunch, she got Ty to drive the trailer out into the yard. "We'll just see what he does," she called, as she went to fetch Star's bridle. She noted that it was made from the best quality English leather. Mr Halliwell, Star's owner, obviously wasn't short of cash.

Star snuffled her pockets as she slipped the bridle over his ears and did up the throat-latch. "He's a good-looking horse," Ty said appreciatively.

Amy guided Star towards the trailer. But as soon as he saw

it, she felt him stiffen. "Walk on." Star stopped still and laid back his ears. "Walk on," she repeated insistently, clicking her tongue to encourage him.

The thoroughbred took another few hesitant steps and then threw up his head and plunged sideways.

"Whoa, steady!" called Ty. "Take it easy, Amy."

Amy nodded, concentrating all her efforts on hanging on to the bridle as the horse threw himself about. "It's OK – calm down, boy!" But it was as if he were possessed. He reared up, his front feet lashing through the air, centimetres from her head.

"Amy!" There was a scream from the kitchen but Amy only vaguely registered it. She jumped out of the way of the angry hooves, and the second Star's feet touched the ground took the opportunity to grab his reins close to the bit and pull him round in a tight circle before he could go up again.

Keeping him circling, she moved him swiftly away from the trailer and brought him to a halt. "OK," she said, looking him in the eye. "So you don't like trailers. I get the message."

"Amy!" Lou came running out of the house. Her blue eyes were wide with fright. "Are you all right? I thought you were going to be killed!" She stopped a little way off, her face ashen.

Amy looked at her in surprise. "He only reared up." Suddenly she remembered that she wasn't talking to Lou. She scowled angrily. "Anyway, what would you care?"

Lou looked as if she had just been slapped in the face. Two

spots of colour sprang to her cheeks and turning abruptly, she marched back down to the house.

Amy noticed Ty's astonished look. She didn't feel like explaining. She turned her attention back to Star. "All right, boy," she said soothingly. "Let's take things slowly." She clicked her tongue and led him back to his stall. *That's what they all needed to do*, she thought. *Take things one step at a time.*

By the time Amy had brushed Star over and settled him in his stall, she was beginning to feel guilty. She kept thinking about the hurt on Lou's face and the way she had stormed back into the house. As Amy put Star's halter away she glanced towards the kitchen. She could see Lou through the window. Impulsively, Amy hurried down the yard.

Lou glanced round as she heard the back door open. Seeing Amy, her face immediately stiffened.

"Lou..." Amy said uncomfortably.

"What?" Lou snapped. Her eyes were cold.

The words rushed out of Amy. "I'm sorry about what I said — out there, with Star." She looked at Lou expecting to see her expression soften, but it didn't. Lou just stood there, colour mounting in her cheeks. "I ... I didn't mean it," Amy said.

Anger and humiliation darkened Lou's eyes. "But that's the problem, Amy — I really think you did!" Turning on her heel she strode out of the kitchen, slamming the door behind her.

The sound echoed around the kitchen. Amy stared at the

door in shock. Lou had rejected her apology! Humiliation and hurt filled her. She angrily threw back her shoulders. Well, if that was the way Lou wanted to play it, she thought, then fine – *just fine!*

Amy spent most of the rest of the day sitting with Sugarfoot in his stable, working on his ears and grooming his coat in a desperate attempt to make him feel better. Ty stopped by every so often and sat with her for a while. To Amy's relief he didn't bring up the subject of Lou and instead simply talked about Sugarfoot and what else they could do to help the little Shetland.

Late in the afternoon, Sugarfoot drifted off to sleep. Amy kissed him on the nose and crept out of his stable. She would let him rest and use the break to start her work with Star.

Putting a halter and a long-line on the thoroughbred she led him into the small ring. "Now, you and I are going to do some bonding," she told Star, rubbing his forehead. She unclipped the long-line and, stepping back, gently flicked him with the end of it on his hindquarters. "Out you go."

Snorting in surprise, Star shied slightly to the side. Amy clicked her tongue and swung the rope in his direction. Star set off at a trot round the ring. He broke into a canter as she pitched the line at him. She kept him going by clicking her tongue and raising the long-line in his direction every time he looked like he was about to stop.

Amy knew she had to get Star to trust her. To do that, she had to show him that she would listen to him and that she understood him. She was going to "join-up" with him. Amy had watched Marion do it a hundred times but this was the first time she had tried it on her own. She took a deep breath and concentrated on Star.

Her eyes on his eyes, her shoulders square with his head, she drove him round the ring. After six times round she let him slow, and by moving her left shoulder got him to change direction before setting him off again. She watched his inside ear. It stopped moving and seemed to fix on her. When she saw that, she knew she had his respect. His head tipped slightly and he started to lick around his mouth, making chewing movements. With a flick of the line, Amy kept him going a little bit longer and at last he gave her the signal she had been looking for. Stretching out his neck, he lowered his head until it was near the floor. Amy felt a shiver of delight. That was his way of saying that he wanted to be a team with her.

She dropped her eyes, coiled the rope and stood at an angle to him. Star slowed down and stopped. From out of the corner of her eye she could see him looking at her. She held her breath and then let it out as he started walking towards her. When he reached her, he stretched out his neck and touched her shoulder with his muzzle, snorting gently. Amy turned round slowly and rubbed him between the eyes. She felt an electricity buzzing through her. He had joined-up.

By coming in, Star had told her that he trusted her.

Just to check, she walked away. Star followed her. She walked in a circle to the right and then a circle to the left. Star stayed beside her. She tried running and he trotted. She halted and he halted too. At last she turned and stroked his neck and rubbed his forehead again. She clipped his line back on. A couple more times and she would try him in the trailer.

When Amy went into the house for supper that night she took some books with her. Sugarfoot's condition was getting worse. Although he had continued to accept the rescue remedy from her hand he was showing no real signs of improvement. She knew that natural remedies took time to work but a horrible thought just kept repeating in her head — *how much time did Sugarfoot actually have left?*

She sat down in the empty kitchen and opened one of the books. Maybe there was something else that might be more effective, something she hadn't tried yet. She flicked through the pages. Just then Lou walked in. Seeing Amy, she paused rather uncertainly by the door. Amy ignored her.

"Are ... are you still looking for something to help Sugarfoot?" Lou asked, seeing the books.

Amy shut the book she was reading with a thud and got to her feet.

"How is he?" Lou's eyes hesitantly searched Amy's face.

"Don't bother pretending you care!" Amy said bitterly,

heading for the door. "You've made it perfectly clear how you feel about the horses — and me!"

"Amy!" Lou exclaimed. She ran a hand through her hair. "Look! This is ridiculous. I'm just trying to be sensible." Her voice rose. "Someone round here's got to be!"

"Sensible!" Amy cried. "If we were sensible all the time, Mom would never have started this place!" Glaring at Lou, she turned and stalked out of the room.

Chapter Eight

"He's not looking good." Ty shook his head and looked at Amy with worried eyes. They were standing side by side in Sugarfoot's stall, staring down at the Shetland.

With every breath he took, he made a wheezing noise and a thick discharge ran from his nostrils. This was the very sign they didn't want. "He's getting too weak to fight," Amy said anxiously. "I'm going to ring Scott."

She hurried down to the house to make the phone call. Although it was still early in the morning, Scott was immediately alert. "I'll be with you within the hour."

Amy returned to the barn. "He's on his way." She looked down at Sugarfoot and as she watched his laboured breathing, she felt her eyes fill up with tears.

"I'll feed the other horses," Ty said, squeezing her arm. "You just stay here."

Amy nodded and knelt down beside Sugarfoot. He sighed and coughed and rested his head listlessly on the straw.

When Scott arrived, he had an expression of deep concern on his face. He shook his head when he'd listened to Sugarfoot's breathing. "It's broncho-pneumonia," he said, straightening up after his examination. "As I suspected, his immune system is severely weakened." He rubbed his forehead with his hand. "Amy," he sighed, "there's a strong chance we're going to lose him."

Amy stared at him in dismay. "But there must be something you can do!"

"I'll give him the appropriate drugs, of course," Scott said, "but they aren't going to be enough to keep him alive. He's lost his will to live."

Amy looked at the little pony. She couldn't bear it. "I won't let you give up, Sugarfoot!" Determination filled her. She didn't care what it took. She was going to keep him alive.

After Scott had injected Sugarfoot with antibiotics and pain-killers and taken a sample of mucus for laboratory analysis, he and Amy left the stall. "Keep him warm and quiet and carry on trying to get him to eat. Ring me if there's any change; otherwise, I'll come again tomorrow." He looked curiously at Star as they passed the front barn. "New horse?"

"Yes, he came yesterday. He's here to be cured of his fear of trailers," Amy explained.

"He's a looker," Scott said. He walked curiously up to the stall. "You know, he seems familiar. Who does he belong to?"

"A man called Nick Halliwell," Amy said, patting Star.

"Halliwell!" Scott exclaimed. "You mean *the* Nick Halliwell?"

Amy shrugged.

"Amy," Scott said, looking at her as if she were mad. "Nick Halliwell is the famous show-jumper." Scott saw Amy's eyes widen. "Yes, that one. He moved into the county a couple of months ago. I've been over to his yard a few times. I thought I recognized Star. He's the talk of the yard — a future Olympic horse, or so Nick says."

Amy stared at Scott in amazement. She had one of Nick Halliwell's horses here in front of her. Nick Halliwell, show-jumping genius. "He said Star was special but I just thought he meant special to him," she said incredulously.

Scott shook his head.

"Wow!" Amy said, looking at Star with new eyes. "Wow!"

Scott grinned. "So how's it going with him?"

Amy explained about Star's reaction to the trailer and then her joining-up session. "It went really well. I was going to try again today but..." she thought about Sugarfoot, "well, with Sugarfoot being so bad, I think I'd better stay with him."

"Sugarfoot just needs to rest," Scott said. "Carry on with your other work as normal." He glanced at his watch. "I don't have to be anywhere for another hour yet. Can I watch you working with Star?"

"OK," Amy agreed. "I'll go get the long-line."

Scott leant against the fence as Amy went through the process of joining-up again with Star. It was a relief, in a way, to be able to focus so entirely on Star and escape from her anxiety about Sugarfoot for a short while. Star only cantered round twice before lowering his head and chewing and licking with his mouth. Amy turned to let him come in to her. He nuzzled her shoulder and then followed her round the ring as he had done the day before.

She stopped and stroked his neck. He lifted his face to hers and blew down his nostrils at her. "What do you think?" she said proudly, clipping the long-line on and leading Star over to Scott.

He climbed over the fence and stopped beside her. "I think you've got your mom's touch," he said, his eyes warm.

Amy felt tears prick at the back of her eyes and she looked down. Scott hugged her. "She'd be so proud of you," he said softly.

Amy swallowed the hard lump of tears in her throat. Sensing her distress, Star nudged against her, rubbing his face on her arm, his dark eyes looking at her with surprise and concern. She smiled through her tears and patted him.

"So what's the next step with him?" Scott asked.

Amy brushed the tears away from her eyes and focused on

Star. "I guess now I need to see how he reacts to the trailer," she said. "Hopefully he'll trust me this time round."

She checked her pockets for treats. It was important that if Star did trust her enough to go into the trailer or even to go near the trailer that she could reward him and make it a pleasant experience.

As they walked Star down the yard to the trailer, Scott said, "I'm going to have another patient for you soon – if you want him."

"Who?" Amy frowned.

"Spartan." Scott saw her puzzled expression. "The bay stallion from the Mallens' farm?" A look of anxiety crossed his face as he saw her start. "Of course, if you don't want him here," he added quickly, "I'm sure we can find somewhere else."

Amy didn't know what to say. The horse that had been the reason for her and Mom going out that day. How would she feel about him? Would she be able to cope?

"You don't have to decide now," Scott said, responding to the turmoil she knew must be reflected in her eyes. "Just bear it in mind, for me. OK?"

Amy bit her lip and nodded.

They reached the area outside the house where the trailer was. Scott let down both the rear and side ramps, and then stood back as Amy let Star follow her round in circles, his head almost touching her shoulder. He looked like a toddler trailing its mom. When she was convinced that he was happy and relaxed, Amy started moving closer to the trailer.

Star snorted, stopped and stepped back. It was his way of saying that he wasn't happy. Amy listened to him and turned into a circle away from the trailer. She glanced at Star. He had stopped and was following her movements with a surprised expression in his eyes. *You listened to me*, he seemed to say. *You actually listened to me!* She walked on and he came trotting after her, slowing to a walk when he was by her shoulder again. This time he stayed even closer than before. After a few more circles, Amy tried again.

This time, Star trusted her enough to follow her around the trailer. After circling it in both directions, Amy walked up the ramp and took a couple of steps into the trailer. Star stopped at the bottom, his front hooves square with the ramp. He lifted his head with a jerk. *That's fine*, Amy showed him by sitting down on the edge of the ramp, taking a carrot out of her pocket and biting a piece off the end. *He could take his time*. Star's ears pricked at the sound of the crunch. Looking slightly to the side of him, Amy munched on the end of the carrot. Star snorted and, lowering his head, walked up the ramp and blew into Amy's face.

"Decided to join me, have you?" she smiled, snapping the carrot in two and giving him half. She tried to appear as calm as possible but inside she was jumping up and down with delight. She fed Star the rest of the carrot and then stood up and walked straight through the trailer and out the other side. With just the slightest hesitation, Star followed her.

She stroked his neck and immediately led him through again. This time there was no hesitation.

As she brought Star to a halt a good distance from the trailer, Scott came striding over. "Well done!"

Amy put her arms round Star's neck and hugged him hard. "He's brilliant!" she said, her eyes shining with happiness.

Scott smiled. "He's not the only one."

After Scott had left, Amy put Star away and hurried to find Ty to tell him the good news. He was mucking out one of the stalls in the back barn. "Of course, he's not properly cured yet – I want to go through it lots more times with him and then he's got to learn to go in with other people – but isn't it good?" Amy gabbled excitedly.

Ty nodded, grinning at her. "I bet his owner will be pleased."

"And guess who that is?" Amy said with a hint of pride in her voice. She paused. "Nick Halliwell!"

Ty was just as astonished as she had been. "The show-jumper?"

"Yes!" Amy said. "It didn't occur to me – he just sounded really normal on the phone." Suddenly she heard a dry, rasping cough coming from Sugarfoot's stall. The excitement that had been bubbling through her dried up instantly.

"Sugarfoot," she said, going quickly over to the stall and looking over the door.

There was no apparent change in the little horse's condition. His breathing was still laboured and with every breath he took a wheeze rasped out of him.

Ty joined her in the stall. "Some tea-tree oil might help clear his passages," he said. "That worked well on Topper last winter. And if we could get some garlic or black sampson down him, they would help the infection."

"I'll see what I can do," Amy said.

She dropped a few drops of undiluted tea-tree oil on to a pad of cotton wool and held it just under Sugarfoot's nose, being careful not to let it touch his muzzle in case it irritated his skin. After a few minutes, she took it away and offered Sugarfoot some of the herbs Ty had suggested but Sugarfoot turned his head. Amy sighed with frustration. The herbs would help him fight his infection but not if he didn't eat them. Amy stayed with Sugarfoot all morning, massaging his ears and face. Every so often she would stop to offer him something to eat, but with no luck.

At lunchtime, Ty came into the stall. "You need a rest," he said.

"I'm fine," Amy replied. She was determined not to leave Sugarfoot.

Ty frowned. "You're not fine," he said firmly. "You need to eat something and get some fresh air. Come and have some lunch." Amy looked at him in surprise. She wasn't used to him ordering her around. But Ty's tone was adamant and Amy reluctantly gave in.

"Are you going to work Star again later?" he asked as they went into the kitchen and found some lunch things.

"Um ... I don't know." Amy's thoughts were occupied with Sugarfoot.

"I think you should," Ty said. "You should reinforce what he did this morning."

Amy knew that Ty was right. "I guess so," she said.

He raised his eyebrows. "You *know* so."

After they'd eaten, Amy got Star out of his stall to repeat what she had done that morning. Soon the chestnut horse was following her quite happily in and out of the trailer.

Ty watched. "He's looking good!"

Amy smiled. "Do you want to try?"

With Ty leading him and Amy walking on his other side, Star walked up into the trailer again. By the time Amy called a halt to the session Star would quite happily allow Ty to lead him in and out of the trailer on his own. Amy was thrilled. It was a major step. Her work would have been useless if Star would only go in the trailer for her. The next move would be to start putting the ramp up when he was inside.

"I think that's enough for today," she said, anxious to get back to Sugarfoot. "Let's stop on a good note."

However, just as she had put Star away in his box, a

large silver car came purring up the drive. "Who's that?" Ty said.

Amy frowned. "I don't know…" She broke off. "Oh, yes, I do," she said, her heart sinking as the car drew nearer and she caught sight of the girl with long ash-blonde hair sitting in the front passenger seat. "It's Ashley and her mom."

"Ashley Grant?" Ty said, recognizing the name of Amy's show-jumping rival. "From Green Briar?"

Amy nodded. "I wonder what they want?"

The car drew to a halt. Val Grant, a large woman with short blonde hair and legs clad tightly in navy breeches, got out. Amy swallowed and went over. "Hello, Mrs Grant."

Val Grant smiled. It was a smile that seemed to contain too many perfect white teeth. "Amy," she said. "How are you?"

"OK," Amy said, wondering what she wanted.

Ashley got out of the car too. She leant against the door frame, her shining hair falling over her shoulders. "Hi, Amy."

"Hi," Amy said briefly.

"We were so sorry to hear about your mom," Val Grant said solicitously. "We thought we'd stop by and see how you were. How have you been coping?"

"Fine, thank you," Amy replied politely, thinking they were the last people she would share her problems with. Mrs Grant didn't seem to be listening, though; she was glancing round the yard as if looking for something.

Val Grant turned her attention back to Amy. "There's a

rumour going round that you've got one of Nick Halliwell's horses here." She sounded casual but her eyes were needle-sharp.

So that's why you're here! Amy thought to herself. She took great pleasure in nodding and seeing Ashley's and Mrs Grant's facial muscles tighten. "Yes. He's in the stall over there." With perfect timing Star put his head out over the stall door.

"Oh," Ashley said, surprised. She walked over to the stall and stroked Star. As she did so, she smiled at Ty who was standing a little way off. "Hello," she said.

"So who's treating him?" Mrs Grant said to Amy.

"I am," she replied.

Val Grant looked as if she couldn't believe what she had just heard. "I see." She cleared her throat. "Well, if you need a hand, just let me know. Ashley!" she called. "Let's not bother Amy any longer!"

With a last lingering smile at Ty, Ashley sauntered back to the car. She got in without even saying goodbye. *So much for caring how I am*, thought Amy cynically.

Val Grant paused as she opened the driver's door. "How about your other horses? Are you managing to cope with all of them?"

Amy nodded. "Yes, thanks. We're just fine."

Val Grant nodded thoughtfully and then got into the car. Amy watched them drive away. Shaking her head she went back to Ty.

"Mm, nice family," he commented, raising an eyebrow.

"Not!" Amy said.

Amy sat with Sugarfoot for the rest of the day. In the early evening, Ty came to find her. "I'm off now," he said. "Is there any change in him?"

Amy shook her head. Sugarfoot's breathing was still heavy and his temperature was high. "But I'm not going to give up." She pushed her hand through her hair. "There has to be something we can do."

Ty looked at her with concern and understanding. "Don't stay in here all night. You look worn out."

"I won't." Amy sighed. "See you tomorrow."

When he'd gone, Amy set to work again, gently massaging Sugarfoot's face with neroli oil. As her fingers worked she focused her mind on willing him to get better. "I'm going to keep trying," she told him. "I'm determined that you're going to get through this, Sugarfoot." But his head remained resting on the straw. It was as if he had put up an invisible barrier and nothing that Amy did would reach him.

Amy was so absorbed in her work that she hardly noticed the lengthening shadows on the stall floor as late afternoon turned to evening. Her temples began to throb with the effort of concentrating for so long and she rested her head against Sugarfoot's neck.

"Amy." She looked up. Grandpa had come home. "I think

you should come in now, honey. You've given it your best shot."

Frustration welled up inside Amy. "What good is my best shot if it hasn't made Sugarfoot better?" she said angrily.

"Amy. Come on." Seeing her grandpa's unwavering expression, Amy reluctantly got to her feet and left the stall without saying a word. On her way down to the house she collected an armful of battered books from the feed-room. Maybe she had missed something. There just *had* to be more she could do to help Sugarfoot.

Chapter Nine

"Amy! Phone!" Ty called up the yard.

Amy started. It was mid-afternoon the following day. Apart from a brief time spent working Star, she had hardly left Sugarfoot's side. The Shetland coughed, his whole body shaking with the effort. *He's getting worse*, she thought with a dreadful sinking feeling in her heart. She felt his ears. The sky was overcast outside and the air was cool, but Sugarfoot's ears were damp and hot.

Ty came hurrying up to the stall door. "Nick Halliwell is on the phone."

Amy got to her feet. Her head ached and her eyes were hurting. She had read far into the night, desperately searching for some remedy that might help Sugarfoot, but she had found nothing. She went down to the house.

"Hi," she said, picking up the receiver. "Amy Fleming here."

"Hello, Amy," said Nick. "I was calling to find out how Star was doing?"

Amy leant against the wall. Account books were spread out across the kitchen table – pages of tiny figures and columns with calculations. "Fine." She forced herself to concentrate. "Good, actually. He went into the trailer and let us put the ramp up this morning. Tomorrow, I'm…"

Nick interrupted. "You've got him into a trailer?"

"Yes," Amy said. "He's walking in quite happily now. He's still not completely cured – that will take a little more time – but he's definitely on the way."

"You've had him two days and you say that he's already walking easily up a ramp?" Nick sounded incredulous. "With no problem?"

"Yes," Amy repeated patiently.

"This I have got to see!"

"Well, as I said, he's not really ready to come home just yet," Amy said quickly. "We need to get him used to being in the trailer while the van's moving and for longer periods of time."

"But can I come and see him walking up the ramp?"

"Sure," Amy replied.

"This is great news. I'll be over in half an hour."

"What? Now?" Amy's eyes widened. "It's not really a good time," she began hastily. "You see…"

But Nick Halliwell didn't seem to be the sort to take no for an answer. "I won't stay long," he interrupted. "I just want a quick look. Right. Half an hour. See you then."

Amy replaced the phone. This was just what she didn't need. Star hadn't even been groomed! At that moment, Lou came into the kitchen, a calculator in her hand. "Hi," she said.

Amy gave her a stony look in reply.

"We've had some good news," Lou said, smiling. "Val Grant just called. She's offered to help us with a couple of the horses until we get things sorted out. She's going to take Pegasus, Sundance and Jasmine."

Amy gasped in horror.

"What's the matter?" Lou said, frowning as she saw her reaction.

"She's not having them!" Amy cried.

"Why not?" Lou looked confused.

"Because of the way she treats her horses! No way, Lou! Absolutely not!"

"Oh, Amy, she can't be that bad," Lou said, raising her eyebrows. "It would be the sensible thing to do and then she might want to have them permanently – buy them, maybe – which would be a real help."

"Never!" Amy almost exploded with rage. "How can you even consider letting Daddy's horse go?"

"But Amy…"

Amy ran from the kitchen, slamming the door as hard as she could behind her.

Ty was waiting for her by Sugarfoot's stall. "Hey! What's up?" he said in alarm as she stormed up the yard.

Suddenly Amy couldn't help herself. She was too tired, too full of emotion. Burying her head in her hands she burst into tears. Ty stepped forward and took her in his arms. "Hey, come on," he soothed. "Tell me what happened. Why are you upset?"

Amy sobbed out Lou's latest plans. "I hate her, Ty! I really do hate her! She's going to ruin everything!"

Ty stroked her hair. "Come on, now, that's crazy. Everything will be OK."

"How can it be?" Amy cried. "Grandpa, you and I can't cope on our own! Lou just wants to go back to New York! What are we going to do?"

"Something will turn up," Ty said, still stroking her hair. "You'll see." He held her until her sobs quietened. At last, she sniffed. "I've made your T-shirt all wet," she said, stepping back and feeling slightly embarrassed.

"That's all right," Ty said quietly. He looked at her with a concerned smile. "So what did Nick Halliwell want?"

Amy's eyes widened as she remembered. "He wants to come and see Star *now*! Can you give him a brush over for me, Ty?"

"Well, actually," Ty shifted his feet, looking a bit embarrassed, "I was kind of on my way." Amy suddenly noticed that he had changed out of his yard clothes. "It's my half-day today," he said as if to remind her. "I know I haven't been taking them recently but I need to get some groceries and things in at home."

Amy immediately felt dreadfully guilty. She'd completely forgotten that Ty normally had a half-day once a week. He'd been working so hard.

"I'll stay if you want," he offered.

"No, of course not," Amy said quickly, her hand flying to her temples as they resumed their throbbing. "You've been brilliant, Ty. You go home."

"Everything's done. The feeds are ready and the stalls are all clean." He stepped towards her, his eyes anxious. "Now, are you sure you'll be OK?"

"Sure." Looking up into his worried face, she smiled — words leaping impulsively out of her. "Thanks for everything, Ty," she said. "You've been a real friend."

There was a pause. Ty's eyes searched hers and then suddenly, without warning, he reached out, and stroked her cheek. At the tender touch of his warm hand, Amy felt an immense shock run through her.

It was over in a couple of seconds. Ty stepped back. Amy's hand flew to her face, her grey eyes wide with surprise, too astonished to speak.

"See you tomorrow," Ty muttered, and then swinging round he strode quickly away.

Amy stared after him, a storm of emotions overwhelming her — she was shocked by the implications of his action, but she had to admit that she felt a certain delight. Why had he done it? And what did it mean?

"Amy!" she vaguely heard her grandpa calling her from

the house. "Soraya's on the phone!"

Her mind still reeling, Amy set off in a daze down the yard.

"That is amazing!" Nick Halliwell looked on with an expression of astonishment on his face as Amy led Star out of the trailer for the third time. He looked just like he did on TV – blond hair, sun-tanned face and sharp blue eyes. When she had first seen him get out of his car, she had felt a sudden rush of butterflies in her stomach but now, with Star to concentrate on, her nerves had left her.

"Well, like I said on the phone, he's still got a little way to go but it's a good start," she said, leading Star over. The horse quickened his pace as he approached his owner and nibbled his outstretched palm.

"A *good* start? It's more than I ever hoped for." Nick vigorously patted the horse's chestnut neck. "You've worked a miracle," he said to Amy. He looked her up and down. "How old are you?"

"Fifteen," she replied.

He shook his head. "Well, you've done more than anyone else has ever been able to do with this horse and like I said, he's a special boy." He smiled at her. "By the time I've passed the word round about this, you're going to be overwhelmed with horses." He smiled. "You'd better get building another barn."

Amy's throat tightened at the unfairness of it all. Build

another barn! Not if Lou had her way. A sudden aching depression filled Amy as she looked at the barn and the fields to the side and beyond. If Lou's plan came off then all this was going to change. The fields and barns would no longer be full of horses. Heartland wouldn't be there to help those that needed their help the most. Horses like Sugarfoot and Star.

Nick didn't seem to notice her quietness. He patted her on the shoulder. "Well, I don't want to hold you up. Thanks for letting me have a look. When can I expect him home?"

Amy forced down her emotion. "In about ten days," she said. "I'll let you know."

"OK. Keep up the good work!" Giving Star one last pat, Nick Halliwell strode down the yard to his car.

Amy watched him drive off. "Star," she whispered, burying her face in the horse's neck and giving way to the wave of tiredness that swept over her. "Why is life so complicated?" She heard the back door open and looked round.

Lou was coming out. She hesitated for a moment and then walked over. "I was watching from the kitchen window," she said, stopping a distance away from Star. She looked uncomfortable. "I just wanted to say well done. You've ... you've done a really good job."

For Amy, it was the last straw. "Well, thank you, Lou!" Hot anger shot through her. "Like you really care!" she cried. Rage, misery and exhaustion consumed her. "If things turn out your way then Heartland will never help another horse!"

Lou took a step forward. "Amy..."

"Don't touch me!" Amy hissed. "If you cared you'd be staying to help us keep it open rather than trying to close it down. But you don't care about anything that really matters!" Amy was shaking with emotion now. "You don't care about Grandpa or me or the horses! And as for Mom – have you even noticed that she's dead?" Acting blindly, without thinking, she grabbed Star's mane and the next instant she was on his back.

"Amy!" Lou's voice rose with alarm. "Amy, stop! What are you doing?"

"Getting as far away from you as possible!"

With a sob, Amy dug her heels into Star's side. He leapt forward and with just one lead-rope to guide him, she galloped him bareback up past the fields and on to the trail that led into the woods. On and on she went, her mind blank apart from the desperate need to escape, to run away. She didn't stop until she had put several kilometres between her and the house. Only then did she notice Star's laboured breathing and sweating sides.

She let him slow to a walk and then to a halt. Suddenly Amy became horribly aware of what she had done. Star didn't even belong to her. Her heart pounding, she slipped off his back. He was breathing heavily, his nostrils moist and flaring. She crouched down and quickly checked his legs. Relief flooded through her as she realized there was no obvious damage. She didn't even like to think how valuable Star was. If she had injured him in any way...

She threw her arms round the chestnut's hot, damp neck. "Oh, Star, I'm so sorry." He nuzzled her and snorted. She rubbed his head and looked around. Where were they? They had come off the trail a long way back. The trees towered overhead. From high above she could just hear the first pattering of rain falling. She shivered. Her bare arms felt cold.

She remounted and, clicking her tongue, turned Star and headed back through the trees the way they had come. But after a few minutes it was impossible to work out which path they had taken. There were so many forks in the track. When they passed what looked like the same fallen tree for about the fourth time, Amy felt panic starting to set in. How were they ever going to find the way back home?

As they reached yet another fork in the path, Amy looked from left to right. She dropped the lead-rope on Star's neck in despair. Which way? She really didn't have a clue. Star stepped towards the left track, his ears pricked. Amy was about to check him but stopped herself. Was it possible that he knew the way back? Sitting very still and dropping all commands, she let him pick his way through the trees.

She was just beginning to give up hope that the thoroughbred really did know the way, when suddenly he stepped out of the trees on to the trail. Relief rushed through her, and leaning forward to throw her arms around Star's neck, Amy burst into tears.

Afternoon was fading into evening and rain drizzled from

the sky, soaking Amy's T-shirt and jeans, but she didn't care. They were almost home.

As she neared the gate, Lou came running up the yard. Amy's heart sank. Now she was going to get it. "I'm sorry," she burst out, jumping off Star and clutching on to his lead-rope with her cold hands. "I'm really sorry, Lou." She looked at Lou, expecting her to explode with anger. Instead she saw that Lou's eyes were wide and frightened.

"Amy!" she gasped. "It's Sugarfoot ... I think he's dying.'

Chapter Ten

Hastily shutting Star in his loose box, Amy raced up to the back barn, her heart pounding. She looked over the half-door. The little pony was lying flat out on the straw, his eyes closed. Lou had covered him with a blanket. "Little Sugarfoot," Amy half sobbed. Opening the door, she crouched beside him and very gently stroked his neck and face. "Please don't die. Please get better." And then, no longer able to control herself, great, racking sobs tore through her.

"I've called Scott," Lou said. She stood uncertainly in the stall doorway. "He's on his way."

Amy nodded in recognition.

"What about Star?" Lou said.

"Star?" Amy suddenly remembered that Star was standing cold and damp in his loose box. "He needs rubbing down." She half stood up and then knelt down again to stroke Sugarfoot's neck once more. She couldn't bear to leave him.

"I'll do it," Lou said suddenly. "You stay here."

Amy turned, shocked. But Lou was already hurrying down the yard. Just then, Sugarfoot coughed. Amy's eyes flew back to him. Stroking his neck, she started to shiver in her damp clothes.

A little while later, she heard a motor engine and the sound of a car door. Quick footsteps strode up the yard. She looked round as Scott entered the stall. "Amy," he said in a hushed voice, kneeling down beside her. He didn't say any more as he checked Sugarfoot over. Amy felt her eyes fill up with fresh tears.

Lou appeared in the stall doorway. She was carrying a mug of coffee, a fleecy top and a blanket. "Here," she said to Amy. "You're soaked through." Amy's fingers were so cold that she could hardly pull the top over her head. She gulped at the hot coffee, barely tasting it.

"I found him like this about half an hour ago," Lou said to Scott. "I put down some fresh straw and tried to keep him warm."

"You did just the right thing," Scott said, looking at her square in the face for the first time.

"Is there anything you can do?" Lou asked.

Scott stroked Sugarfoot's neck. "Well, I could give him more injections to fight any infection and stop the pain, but that's about all." He stood up and sighed. "He's in a really bad way," he said, rubbing a hand over his eyes. "It might be for the best if we put him to sleep."

"What?" Amy said through trembling lips.

"We can't let him suffer," Scott replied. "He's been through enough."

"You said you could give him painkillers. He might still get better!" Tears choked Amy's voice as she looked down at the little Shetland stretched out in the straw.

Scott crouched down beside her and put his hands on her shoulders. "More medicine is not the answer. He just doesn't want to get better, Amy," he said gently. "That's the problem. He's not fighting to stay alive any more. If he was, then there would be hope. But he's given up."

"Just one more night!" Amy begged frantically. "Just give us one more night!"

Scott looked at her for a long moment. "OK," he said at last. "One more night." He got up to prepare an injection for Sugarfoot. A few minutes later, as he left, he turned to Lou. "I'll be round first thing tomorrow morning. Give me a call if there's any change."

She nodded. "I will." She smiled gratefully at him. "Thank you for coming so quickly, Scott. It means a lot – to both of us."

"No problem." Scott looked at her again; his voice was warm. "See you tomorrow, then."

* * *

Amy sat in Sugarfoot's stall, gently stroking the little pony's neck. If only he could tell her what he needed. Right now, she felt as if she had failed him. As the evening turned to night, his breathing became shallower. She touched his face. "Sugarfoot," she whispered, tears trickling down her face. "Please tell me. What is it you want?"

The stall door opened. It was Lou. Both she and Grandpa had come up regularly through the evening to see how Sugarfoot was. "Amy, it's getting late," she said softly. "You should go to bed."

Amy shook her head. "I have to stay with Sugarfoot."

Lou knelt down beside him. "Let me stay with him."

Amy looked at her in surprise. Her sister looked calm and determined.

Lou nodded. "You need to rest. Go on in. You can always take over later." She was insistent and Amy gave in, too exhausted to argue any more. She walked numbly back to the house. Her grandfather was waiting in the kitchen.

"How is he?" He registered the expression on her face. "No better?"

Amy shook her head. Grandpa came forward and hugged her tightly to him. Tears spilling from her eyes, she let her head rest against his chest.

Amy sat bolt upright – what time was it? She checked her bedside clock; she had slept for several hours. What if Lou had left the barn, left Sugarfoot on his own to die? She would never be able to forgive herself for sleeping at such an important time.

Amy scrambled out of bed and rushed over to the window. With relief, she saw a light shining out from the back barn. Lou must still be there.

Going downstairs she looked into the kitchen. The radio was on and Grandpa had fallen asleep in the easy chair. She crept quietly past him and went outside. The night air was cool on her face as she hurried up the yard. When she reached the barn she slowed her pace to a walk. Treading as quietly as she could, she approached Sugarfoot's stall.

Lou's voice came floating out but Amy couldn't quite make out the words. She looked over the stall door. Lou was sitting beside Sugarfoot's head, talking to him. Amy was about to push the door open when she realized that Lou's face was streaming with tears.

She paused, shocked. She couldn't remember *ever* seeing Lou cry. She stepped back uncertainly, not knowing how to react.

"Oh, Sugarfoot, what am I going to do?" she heard Lou say, her voice low and despairing. A sob burst from her. "I don't think I can bear it any longer. I've tried to be strong. I've tried to cope. But I miss Mom so much."

Lou started to cry in earnest. Amy stood frozen to the spot wondering what to do. She thought about saying something, but somehow, something held her back.

Through her tears, Lou started speaking again. "Mom

always said I was the strong one, Sugarfoot, but I just can't deal with it any more." A sob caught in her throat. "I've lost Daddy and I've lost Mom. There's no one I can talk to now. Grandpa and Amy think I don't care, but they don't understand. I'm just trying to keep a brave face. They need me to be strong."

Amy's eyes widened as she listened to Lou's words. *Poor Lou*, she thought in horror. *I never realized*.

"You understand, don't you, Sugarfoot?" Lou said. There was a silence. "I could lose Amy, too. And I can't let that happen ... I just *can't*."

Amy crept forward to look through a chink in the stall wall. Lou was cradling Sugarfoot's head on her knees. Her voice choked with tears, she started to sing softly to the little pony.

After a few seconds, Lou's voice trailed off. "You could be happy here," she said softly. "There are fields, fresh hay, cool, shady trees, and people to love and care for you." She kissed him gently. "I know you lost your mom, Sugarfoot. But Amy and I have lost ours, too. We understand. This could be home for all of us." She started to sing again.

Through her own tears, Amy suddenly noticed that Sugarfoot was stirring, his eyes were flickering. She stared. The singing somehow seemed to be getting through to him. *Of course! That was it!* Mrs Bell had always sung as she worked – it obviously reminded Sugarfoot of home and comforted him. At that moment, the little Shetland weakly lifted his head.

With a gasp, Lou stopped singing, her face shocked. "Sugarfoot!" she whispered. The tiny pony looked at her for a long, long moment. Then slowly and with a great effort, he reached out to touch Lou's arm with his muzzle. "Hello, boy," Lou whispered shakily. She touched his head and he snorted gently. "Did you like that song?"

Lou picked up the herbs that Amy had taken to his stall earlier. She offered him some and to Amy's amazement he started to eat. Picking up a handful, Lou started to sing softly again to him and then as he finished them, she reached for his feed bucket. Handful by slow handful, she fed him the contents — the bran, the barley, the carrots and apples. At last, Sugarfoot turned away.

Lou put down the pail. "Now sleep," she said softly. "Get some rest, little horse. We'll face tomorrow together."

Sugarfoot rested his muzzle on the straw and closed his eyes, and Amy slipped quietly into the stall.

Lou started. "Amy!" Her expression immediately became alarmed and defensive. "How long have you been there?" she asked in a low voice.

Amy hesitated, for a moment wondering whether to lie — but she had heard too much. She met Lou's eyes and tears welled up in her own. Putting her arms round Lou's neck, she cried, "I'm sorry for all those things I said. I'm sorry I said you didn't care. I just didn't understand."

Lou hugged her back. "It's all right," she soothed. "Amy, it's all right."

Amy pulled away. "No, it's not all right! I should have realized. And you've made Sugarfoot better, too," she said, looking at the little Shetland, sleeping at last. "I watched him eating."

Lou's eyes shone. "He just suddenly seemed to wake up. I didn't do anything. Not really."

"But you did!" Amy said passionately. "Don't you see? You understood what he was going through. You sang to him like Mrs Bell used to and reminded him that once he had a happy home. You gave him a reason to start fighting again." For a moment, Amy and Lou both looked at the little pony. "And I thought you hated horses," Amy said.

"I've never hated them," Lou said quickly. "I've just blamed them for all the losses in my life. And being with them brings back so many memories. But I'm beginning to see that you can't run away from your past." She smiled as Sugarfoot snorted into the straw. "And now this little fellow has taught me that you should never give in to your pain." She laid a hand on his head. "I'll miss him when I go back to New York," she said softly. She looked round. "And I'll even miss Heartland."

"Then don't go back," Amy said impetuously. "Stay here. Stay here and help us to keep it going. You could help Ty and me. I could teach you all Mom's techniques. Together we could make it work."

"Oh, Amy, I can't," Lou said, shaking her head. "I live in New York."

"But this is your home!" Amy exclaimed. "You told Sugarfoot that!" She saw the truth of this sink in. "I heard you, Lou. You said we could all live here together."

Lou wavered. "But where will we get the money from? No one's going to bring horses to Heartland now Mom isn't here."

"But they will!" Amy quickly told Lou about Nick Halliwell and what he'd said that afternoon after he'd seen Star. "He'll tell everyone he knows!" She grabbed Lou's hands. "We can do it, Lou!" she said. "We really can!"

Lou was silent for the moment. "We'll never get along. We're too different. We'll fight."

"We'll make up again," Amy said. "I'll be practical. I'll be sensible."

Lou laughed. "You couldn't be if you tried."

"Well, maybe not," Amy admitted with a grin. "But at least I will try." She looked at Lou. "Just please say you'll stay. Please!"

They heard the straw rustle behind them. They both turned. Sugarfoot had lifted his head and was looking at them. The light had come back into his eyes. Amy could see he'd turned a corner; he wanted to live again.

Lou looked from him to Amy. She took a deep breath. "I'm not making any promises," she said. "But for now, I'll stay." She squeezed Amy's hand tightly.

Amy gasped. "Oh, Lou, you don't know what this means to me. You've been away for so long." She flung her arms around her sister's neck. "Thank you for coming home."

Read More about

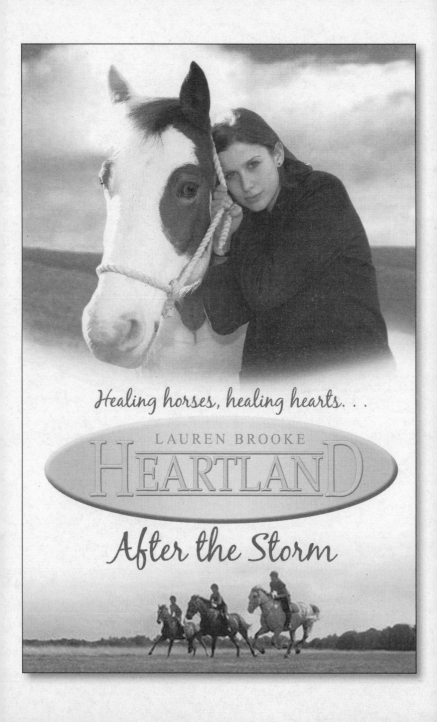

Healing horses, healing hearts. . .

LAUREN BROOKE
HEARTLAND

After the Storm

Healing horses, healing hearts. . .

LAUREN BROOKE

HEARTLAND

Breaking Free

Healing horses, healing hearts. . .

LAUREN BROOKE

HEARTLAND™

Taking Chances

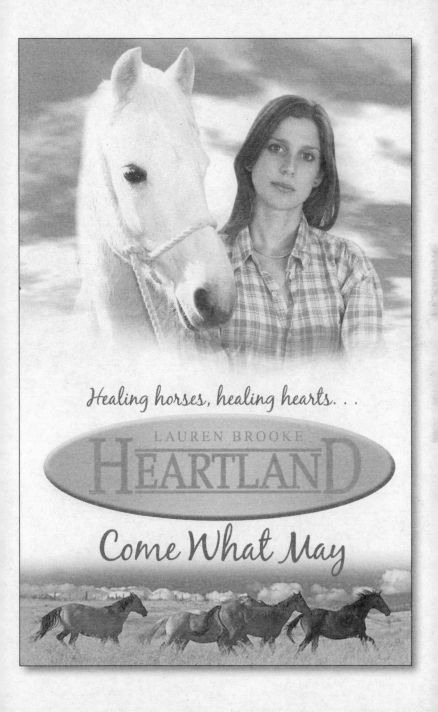

Healing horses, healing hearts. . .

LAUREN BROOKE

HEARTLAND

Come What May

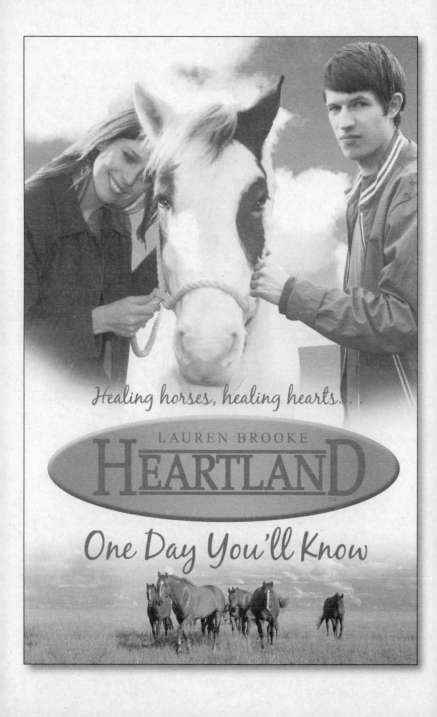

Healing horses, healing hearts. . . .

LAUREN BROOKE

HEARTLAND™

One Day You'll Know

Scholastic Children's Books would like to thank
Vauxhall City Farm for their support and co-operation in
the production of this book. We couldn't have done it
without them or their horses.

Vauxhall City Farm is a charity providing a number of
projects including Riding for the Disabled lessons and
subsidised riding lessons for local inner city children.

History:

Vauxhall City Farm started out in 1977 with local people working voluntarily to transform derelict land into an oasis of country life in the heart of London. The farm attracts people from all around the UK to visit animals that live so near to Big Ben and who are at home in the hustle and bustle of inner London.

On the Farm

The Farm is a sensory experience with smells to accompany the bleating, mooing, neighing and oinking.

A walk through the farm takes you pass the goats and cows, with the help of signs and our committed volunteers, we try to make everyone's experience of the animals as positive and interactive as possible. If you carry on through the farm you reach the duck pond and the community garden.

Just outside the farm you can watch the animals grazing in the paddocks or a riding lesson in the school. Down by the horse paddocks live the chickens and rabbits, with a lovely ecology green space in which to eat your picnic.

Riding centre

We have a horse riding centre which provides subsidised riding lessons for local children, along with Riding for the Disabled and private lessons.

School activities

The Farm provides tours for schools and nursery groups with themes such as animal care, healthy eating and growing.

Vauxhall City Farm has disabled access to all public areas; please call us to for further details and/or book lessons or visits.

Ways to support Vauxhall City Farm:

Donations

Entrance to the farm is free but we depend upon the generosity of all our supporters and we're very grateful to everyone who makes a donation.

Animal Sponsorship

You can sponsor any animal from a guinea pig to a horse for yourself or as a gift. We will send you a certificate.

Corporate Sponsorship

We have several companies who have sponsored the horses and our larger livestock. Our horses give disabled children the chance to experience the joys of riding.

Volunteering

We welcome skilled and non-skilled volunteers, the farm recognises the importance of sharing skills and knowledge. The farm is unique in its volunteering programme, bringing all ages together and creating value in social interaction.

For more information about any of the above please contact
linda.hinds@btconnect.com or vcf@btconnect.com

Vauxhall City Farm,
165 Tyers Street,
London SE11 5HS
0207 582 4204

www.vauxhallcityfarm.org

If you liked Heartland, try this. . .

Chestnut Hill
The New Class

Lauren
Brooke

By the author of *Heartland*

SCHOLASTIC

Chestnut Hill

Making Strides

Lauren Brooke

Chestnut Hill
Heart of Gold

Lauren Brooke

By the author of *Heartland*

◼ SCHOLASTIC

If you liked Heartland, try this. . .

Chestnut Hill
Playing for Keeps

Lauren
Brooke

By the author of *Heartland*

SCHOLASTIC

If you liked Heartland, try this. . .

If you liked Heartland, try this. . .

Chestnut Hill
Team Spirit

Lauren Brooke

By the author of *Heartland*

SCHOLASTIC

If you liked Heartland, try this. . .

Chestnut Hill

All or Nothing

Lauren Brooke

By the author of *Heartland*

Chestnut Hill
Chasing Dreams

Lauren Brooke

By the author of *Heartland*

SCHOLASTIC

If you liked Heartland, try this. . .

Chestnut Hill
A Time to Remember

Lauren
Brooke

By the author of *Heartland*

SCHOLASTIC

If you liked Heartland, try this...

If you liked Heartland, try this. . .

Chestnut Hill
Helping Hands

Lauren
Brooke

By the author of *Heartland*

If you liked Heartland, try this. . .

Chestnut Hill
Racing Hearts

Lauren Brooke

By the author of *Heartland*